Dutch and Gina
The Sins
of the
Fathers

Mallory Monroe

AUSTIN BROOK PUBLISHING

This novel is a work of fiction. All characters are fictitious. Similarities to anyone living or dead are completely accidental. The specific mention of known places or venues are not meant to be exact replicas of those places, but are purposely embellished or imagined for the story's sake.

ISBN:0615685242
ISBN-13:978-0615685243

THE PRESIDENT'S GIRLFRIEND SERIES
IN ORDER

THE PRESIDENT'S GIRLFRIEND

THE PRESIDENT'S GIRLFRIEND 2:
HIS WOMEN AND HIS WIFE

DUTCH AND GINA
A SCANDAL IS BORN

DUTCH AND GINA
AFTER THE FALL

DUTCH AND GINA
THE POWER OF LOVE

THE MOB BOSS SERIES
IN ORDER:

ROMANCING THE MOB BOSS

MOB BOSS 2
THE HEART OF THE MATTER

MOB BOSS 3
LOVE AND RETRIBUTION

AUSTIN BROOK PUBLISHING
ALSO PRESENTS
INTERRACIAL ROMANCE
BY
BESTSELLING AUTHOR

KATHERINE CACHITORIE

LOVING HER SOUL MATE

LOVING THE HEAD MAN

SOME CAME DESPERATE
A LOVE SAGA

AUSTIN BROOK PUBLISHING
PROUDLY PRESENTS

BY

BESTSELLING
AND
AWARD-WINNING AUTHOR

TERESA MCCLAIN-WATSON

AFTER WHAT YOU DID

DINO AND NIKKI
AFTER REDEMPTION

VISIT

www.austinbrookpublishing.com
for updates and more information
on all titles.

PROLOGUE

TWELVE YEARS EARLIER

Dutch Harber stood at the wall-to-wall window that overlooked a panoramic view of Vegas at night. He gulped down the last of his drink as laughter roared in the adjacent room.

"They're waiting for you," Max said as he stared at his long-time friend.

Dutch said nothing. He continued to stare out of that window, and at the swirling nightlife that surrounded the well-placed hotel.

Max looked at that nightlife, too, and then looked at his friend again. "Dutch, they're waiting for you," he said once more.

Dutch finally looked at Max. He was, by far, his oldest and dearest friend. "Care to join us?" he asked with a wicked smile, already certain of the answer.

"Thanks, but no," Max said with a note of distaste in his voice. "Besides, Senator McKenzie hates my guts. He'll choke on his own vomit if I showed my face in there."

Dutch laughed mildly, although, in Max's mind, it was hardly funny. Dutch Harber and Crader McKenzie were both well-respected United States Senators attending a winter retreat for the congressional reelection committee, and were behaving like this. Not funny at all. Boozing and banging, that was all they'd been doing all weekend long. Boozing and banging. And although Dutch would declare he was only slightly tipsy, Max knew he was practically stoned.

Dutch did manage, however, to hand Max his empty glass. Their hands touched in the exchange, with Max gripping Dutch's hand slightly longer than was necessary, as if to keep Dutch with him and out of that room. Dutch felt his friend's momentary grasp, but pulled slightly harder to release his hand. He was no abstainer like Max. He had to have it, and he had to have it repeatedly.

"I'll see you in the morning," he said with what Max thought was a regretful look in his sharp green eyes. And then his tall, lean body headed for the bedroom.

Max stared at that body, at the way he moved so elegantly. Why he wasted his gifts in places like this was a mystery to Max.

But he wasn't so mystified that he mused over it long. He had a job to do. That was his role, after all. He was, if he were to be honest with himself, nothing more than Dutch Harber's clean-up man. He'd played that role since they were kids in boarding school. He always danced to Dutch's tune. Always.

But what was the alternative, he thought as he placed the glass on the hotel's wet bar. Dance to his own tune, and without Dutch? He knew that wasn't a possibility. Dutch Harber was going places, and he was going right along with him.

He proceeded to tidy up the cigarette butts and empty beer bottles and numerous wine glasses that lined the room. This was all in the aftermath of the get together Dutch had thrown earlier for other members of Congress. Max couldn't chance having some cleaning crew see this mess, take pictures, and sell those pictures to the tabloids. Then some tabloid story comes out proclaiming this was how so-called public servants spent their weekends, not to mention how they were spending the American people's tax dollars.

So dutiful Max tidied up the entire room. But he wasn't about to leave the suite. Not yet. He needed insurance. Always had to have that insurance. He pulled out his small, trim-line camera, walked over to the closed bedroom door, and waited.

His wait was short. Because within moments of his arrival at the closed door, Dutch let out one of his loud roars that allowed Max to crack open the bedroom door without being heard.

And there they were. The Honorable Senator Crader McKenzie and The Honorable Senator Walter "Dutch" Harber. Both naked on the bed. Both cocks thick and long and being given serious head by the same gorgeous girl. Beautiful Elvelyn, the blond bombshell Max hand-picked to spend the night with them. She was a good girl from a good family and she knew how to keep her mouth shut.

And she loved to fuck, as long as the guys were hot. Dutch and Crader, even Max had to admit, were scorchers.

And Max took pictures, all sorts of pictures, of their scorch.

They were lying across the bed and she was on her knees on that bed, positioned between both men. Her long, blonde hair kept slinging around her face and she had to keep slinging it back out of her way. And although she would pleasure Crader McKenzie, Max knew she favored Dutch. She'd give Crader a few licks, a mouthful even, but then she kept moving that mouth back to Dutch's massive rod. She'd not only lick Dutch, but would go all the way down on him, and would fill her mouth with that gorgeous pink cock like it was a bite of porterhouse steak. Max licked his lips just imagining how it tasted.

Dutch was laid back, his arms over his forehead, his beautiful eyes closed. He was an Adonis to Max, his ripped abs so taut and tight he looked like the prime pump in a sea of prime pumps. And that massive tool between his legs. It mesmerized Max. So long, so thick, and oh so juicy. And his camera clicked furiously.

But when Dutch suddenly moved Elvelyn to where she was on top of him, and rammed his dick deep inside of her in one swift shove, causing the woman to scream out in ecstasy, Max almost spilled his beans right where he stood.

Crader then got on top of her, ramming his cock up her ass, and they were going at it like sex-starved teenagers, with Dutch easily holding all of their weight. All Max could see of the woman was her legs, sandwiched between these two so-called dignified senators, and they were tapping that thang of hers so hard Crader's own ass was shaking as he pounded her. And these were supposed to be the pillars of their community, Max thought. Two of the most powerful men in the Senate, and among the most powerful in all of the United States. Two sex perverts, if you asked Max.

Dutch and Crader were both nearly drunk, and Elvelyn wasn't far behind, but Max hadn't had a drop of liquor. He was stone cold sober as he watched. As he took his pictures but kept stopping to watch. As he unzipped his pants and kept watching Dutch thrash into that girl, harder and harder, as if she was just his plaything. And Max couldn't take it.

He pulled it out, to release the pressure, and immediately found himself jerking off. He jerked so hard he could hear himself began to grunt it out. He jerked so hard that he soon created a huge puddle of cum at his feet. And it kept pouring out. Because he couldn't stop watching Dutch thrash her. He wanted to be in that girl's position. He wanted it to be him, and not some *got*damn bitch, Dutch was filling up. He wanted to fill up Dutch!

And as soon as that rush of emotion ebbed, and his cum was drained out, and he was just standing there jerking on an empty, limp dick, he was ashamed of himself. Deeply ashamed. He wasn't even gay, for crying out loud! How could he have such dirty, horrible thoughts!

And like every bad turn his life ever took, including this spontaneous act of shame, Max just knew this was all Dutch Harber's fault, too.

CHAPTER ONE

TWELVE YEARS LATER

Dutch stood quietly in the shower stall long after his bath was over. He ran his fingers through his silky black hair and leaned his head all the way back, to absorb the shock of full-forced water as it poured down every curve of his muscular, sinewy body.

He had been at the Helsinki Summit for three days now. Three long days of negotiations by all of the major world leaders and they were no closer to an agreement on Europe's debt crisis than they had been on day one. He missed his wife, he missed his son, he even missed the back and forth of DC politics. At least in Washington he knew where people stood. Here, in Helsinki, Finland, some forty-three hundred miles away, it wasn't even about taking a position. It was all about *not* taking one and wasting everybody's time *not* saying so. Of all the wack-ass duties he had to perform as President of the United States, and there were many, attending these useless summits ranked highest among them.

He turned the water off and prepared to leave the shower. At least today was the last day he planned to remain in town, agreement or no agreement, as those long, drawn-out meetings were set to resume in less than an hour. Problems had better be ironed out today, he had already warned his counterparts, or they weren't going to be ironed out with assistance from the United States. But as soon as he opened the shower door and stepped out onto the bathroom tile, another problem was staring him in the face: His daughter. Jade.

Jade stood in the middle of the hotel's bathroom anxiously anticipating her father's appearance. She was dressed comfortably, in a printed cropped blazer and a pair of white slim-leg pants. The layered curls of her long, brown hair fell over both her shoulders, and her dark green eyes against her light-brown skin gave her a stunning appearance. She knew she was a mixed-race beauty. Her parents, she felt, were both far too attractive for her not to be a looker.

But sometimes she felt unsure of herself. She felt uncomfortable with herself. As if she was a nuisance to everybody who knew her, but they didn't have the guts to tell her so.

When her father stepped out of the shower stall, and saw her standing there, he was startled by the sight. Jade's eyes immediately trailed downward, from his muscular chest and washboard abs, to what she could only describe as his remarkable endowment. But when she saw that he was displeased by her bold appearance in his bathroom, and especially by where her eyes had trailed to, she immediately sprang into action. It was difficult, but a tear did come.

"What's the matter?" Dutch asked as her pretty brown face suddenly became a mask of anguish.

"Oh, *Daddy*," she said tearfully as she hurried to him and fell against his body.

Dutch coolly but firmly took her by the arm and pulled her back, grabbing a towel off of the rack as he did. "What's happened?" he asked anxiously as he wrapped the towel around his well-endowed midsection. "Gina and Little Walt all right?"

Jade could have thrown up when he mentioned Gina's name. That was all he thought about: Gina, Gina, Gina! "They're fine, Daddy. It's not about them."

Dutch stared at his daughter. She was turning out to be a very troubled young lady, and it was beginning to concern him. "Then what is it about?" he asked her.

It took even more effort, but Jade managed to produce more tears. She had learned the trick when she was a child: think about something terrible in her life and the tears would come. Since she had many examples she could draw upon, the tears always came.

"Babe, what is it?" Dutch asked again.

Jade hesitated again, but then she spoke. "I keep thinking about *her*," she said softly.

Dutch remained cool as he watched her. Because he knew what she meant. He took a second towel off of the rack and began rubbing it through his hair, to stop the dripping. Jade looked at his jet-black hair, at his glassy green eyes, at his superfine body. She was certain there couldn't possibly be another man alive better looking than her father. She was proud that she was his.

"The doctor told you, Jade, that it would take significant time," he ultimately said to her.

"But it's been almost a year now. Why am I still thinking about her? It wasn't like she was a real baby. I had a miscarriage. It wasn't like I had her and she was growing up and then she died. I never knew her. I never even saw her. Shouldn't I be over it by now?"

"Of course not," Dutch said softly, alarmed that she didn't realize it herself. "You suffered a terrible loss."

"But it keeps coming back to me. I keep thinking about her. Oh, *Daddy*," Jade said again, summoning the tears again, and fell against his body again.

Dutch placed his towel around his neck and hugged his daughter, rubbing her long, soft hair, attempting to comfort her.

But his mind was unsettled. Gina had privately gone through some therapy sessions last year after the trauma she had endured at the hands of his one-time friend Robert Rand, and the therapist had been excellent. Like Jade, Gina didn't want to talk to anybody, either, believing she didn't need it. But Dutch put his foot down. He told her that she was going to meet with that therapist even if she just sat there and said nothing the entire time.

And that was indeed what stubborn Gina did for the first few sessions. She just sat there and said absolutely nothing, certain Dutch would get the message and tell her she didn't have to go anymore. But he told her she still had to go. And she still went. By session number three she was letting it all out. And feeling better for it. But now, as he held his still-distraught daughter in his arms, he was beginning to wonder if he would have to deploy similar tactics with her.

He pulled her back and looked at her, his hands on her small arms. "We'll talk tonight, all right?"

"Ah, Daddy! Don't tell me you're going to be in meetings all day again!"

"That's why I'm here, Jade. For meetings."

Jade exhaled. This was her first foreign trip with her father, but she rarely saw him.

"Why don't you and Christian go sightseeing?" Dutch suggested as he began walking out of the bathroom. "Do some fun stuff. I have every confidence in the Secret Service. They'll protect you."

"I know they will. It's not that at all. It's just that . . ." She wanted to tell him how she felt, how she truly felt, but her true emotions were never welcomed by anyone. She therefore smiled instead. "Guess who's here?"

Dutch looked back at her. "Here? In Helsinki?"

"Yes."

"Who?"

"Mom's here."

Dutch frowned and stopped walking. "Sam? What in the world is Sam doing here?"

"She came to see you! I've been telling you since forever she wanted to talk to you. But you had all of that craziness going on when the Speaker of the House and then the Vice President resigned. And then LaLa and Uncle Crader got married. And then they promptly had the bad manners to get pregnant, which I think Gina was happier about than when I got pregnant. But anyway. It was just a lot on your plate. And you never made time for Mom." A sadness came into Jade's eyes. Dutch knew how much she cared about her mother.

But it still made no sense to him. "Couldn't it have waited until I returned stateside?" he wanted to know. "Why would she come all the way here?"

Because Gina wouldn't be here to get in between the two of you, Jade wanted to say. "I thought it would be good for her to get away from that ridiculous book store of hers and see the world a little," she said instead. "She agreed and arrived late last night. So I was hoping that maybe you'll make a little time for her before you start your meetings this morning."

It felt like the bum-rush to Dutch and he didn't like it. But he knew Sam well enough to know that she didn't play games. She was odd as hell, but she didn't play games. "I've got to conference with my staff before I attend any of my meetings, so I can't see her this morning. But bring her to the reception this afternoon. I should have some free time then."

Jade was displeased by the fact that she and her mother were never a priority to him, but she pretended as if she was well-pleased. "Oh, thank-you, Daddy!" she said with an exaggerated smile that didn't reach her eyes, and she hugged him again.

And then she was gone.

In a swirl of cheerfulness.

And just like that, Dutch thought, his teary-eyed daughter went from bereaved mother to the happy little lamb she often tried to project herself as being. But that ability of hers, to turn her emotions off and on like a faucet, as if emotions were nothing more than a tool, disturbed him mightily.

"Where's Daddy?" Little Walt asked again as he and his mother hurried out of the South Portico of the White House, and climbed into the waiting limousine.

His mother, Regina "Gina" Harber, smiled. She knew exactly how her son felt. She wanted him back too. "He's still at what they call a summit, honey, in a country called Finland." She said this as she buckled her precocious young son into his car seat. She wasn't going to dumb-down the language for Little Walt. There would be no baby talk from her. She spoke clearly and she answered all of his tons of questions. "He'll be back home late tonight."

"That's not home," Little Walt said as he looked down at the buckle, his shoulder-length, curly brown hair flopping down and around his handsome face.

"What did you say, Walter?"

He jerked his head up, revealing stunningly beautiful green eyes. "Daddy's not home."

"That is absolutely correct," Gina said adoringly as she put on her own seat belt. "You are such a smart little boy. You're smart just like Daddy."

Little Walt, an unusually thoughtful child, scrunched up his face as if he was still trying to work out the sense of his mother's comment. "You say I'm smart like Daddy. Daddy says I'm smart like Mommy." He let out a sigh of great frustration. "I don't know what to believe."

Gina smiled. And then laughed.

The drive to Blair House was a quick one because the residence was a stone's throw from the White House. Although it was known as the president's guest house, Crader McKenzie, who had already taken up temporary residence there before his appointment as vice president, decided to stay until the end of the president's term. He could have moved his family into the official vice presidential residence on the grounds of the Naval Observatory, some three miles away from the White House, but he, instead, stayed put. Which pleased Gina no end. In fact, given the proximity of Blair House to the White House, Gina had wanted to walk over rather than ride. But before Dutch left town he had ordered the Secret Service to not allow her to walk anywhere.

"Surely he didn't mean that to include Blair House," Gina had tried to reason with the agent. "It's right there. It's not even a block away."

But the agent called his boss, his boss called the head of the Secret Service, and the head of the Secret Service decided to phone the president himself for clarification. Dutch then phoned Gina and told her, in no uncertain terms, that she wasn't walking anywhere, and that included Blair House. She wanted to disagree with him but she knew, by his tone, that his word was final on the matter.

Besides, he didn't say she couldn't *go* to Blair House. Just that she couldn't *walk* there. And she needed to get there. They took the limousine.

Crader McKenzie, the Vice President, met them at the Blair House entrance with a grand smile on his handsome face. He was wearing a blue suit, the color matching his eyes, Gina thought, and she had never seen him so ramped-up. He kissed her when she stepped out of the limo, and unbuckled Little Walt himself.

"This is my man right here," Crader said as he lifted Walt into his arms. Walt grinned. "You are just growing by leaps and bounds, little fellar."

"Where's La?" Gina asked.

"Right this way, madam First Lady," Crader said as he escorted Gina and carried Walt into the residence.

Seated in the Eisenhower Room, looking pretty in pink, was Gina's best and oldest friend, Loretta "LaLa" King-McKenzie. And she had her newborn daughter in her arms.

"Baby!" Walt said excitedly as he pointed and smiled when they entered the room.

"Yes," Gina said, even more excitedly. "That's little Nicole. Hello, baby girl," she added as she sat beside La.

"Oh, so I don't exist anymore?" LaLa said with a smile. "It's all about the baby now?"

"All about her, girl," Gina said. "Get used to it."

LaLa and Crader laughed. He took a seat, with Walt on his lap, in the flanking chair.

"Baby doll," Walt said, staring at Nicole.

"Yes, she is," Crader said. "She's my baby doll." Then he thought about it. "What a great nickname for her, La. Baby doll. Let's call her Doll."

LaLa shook her head. This had to be the tenth "nickname" Crader had suggested. "We'll see, dear," she said.

"But really," he said as the double doors to the sitting room opened, "I think it's a great nickname. And we can always give Little Walt credit for being the one to come up with it. It'll be marvelous conversation piece when he and Nicole are playmates together."

LaLa laughed. Crader and this baby. There couldn't possibly be a more attentive father. "We'll see," she said again.

Jeffrey, the usher, complete with white gloves, stepped inside. "Excuse me, Mr. Vice President, but you have a visitor, sir."

"A visitor? Who?"

"The President's chief of staff wishes to see you."

"Allison Shearer?" LaLa asked. "She could have come to the parlor. I haven't had a chance to congratulate her on her promotion anyway. Bring her here, Jeffrey."

"It was suggested, madam," Jeffrey said, "but she prefers his office. It's a matter, she says, of some privacy."

Crader really didn't want to leave his wife and son. Not even for a second. But duty called. "I'd better see what she wants," he said as he stood up and then sat Walt in the chair. "You hold it down for me, big man," he said to the little boy.

Walt frowned, unable to make out exactly what Crader meant. How do you hold down a chair? He wasn't quite sure. But he began pressing his body down into that chair just the same.

When Crader and Jeffrey left the room, Gina looked at LaLa. "He looks so nervous, La," she said with a smile.

"He is. The baby was two months premature, I had eclampsia during the delivery, he's still haunted by all of that. I think he's still a little traumatized."

"My oh my. He is going to spoil you and that baby rotten."

LaLa smiled. "He's doing that already. He rarely goes over to his office at the White House anymore. I can't get rid of him."

Gina laughed. "I never would have thought in a million years that Crader McKenzie would ever settle down and become husband and father the way he has."

"Yes," LaLa agreed. Then a look came over her. It was subtle, but Gina caught it.

"What's wrong, La?"

LaLa hesitated. "It's probably nothing."

"What is it?"

She hesitated again. "He still. . . He still has it in him." She said this and looked at Gina, to see if she understood.

Gina understood. She had married a world renowned playboy herself. "And how do you know this?" she asked her best friend.

20

"I see the way he looks at those attractive women on his staff. And I don't mean a casual glance, either. Sometimes he looks as if he's undressing those women with his eyes, G."

"Knowing Crader, he probably is."

"Gina!" LaLa said. "How can you say that? He's my husband. You don't hear me badmouthing your husband."

"I'm not badmouthing him. I'm telling you the truth. And Dutch probably does the same thing, I'm just keeping it real. We didn't marry a couple of priests, La. We married two virile, *very* virile men. They are going to look."

"But do they touch?"

Gina thought about this. "I can't speak for Crader," she said. "I can only speak for Dutch."

"And I already know your answer," LaLa said. "You're such a realist. I already know you're going to say there's no way of telling if Dutch touches or not. Right?"

"Wrong," Gina said. "You are so wrong. Dutch may look, I know he will look, but he won't touch."

"But you can't be a hundred percent certain of that," LaLa reminded her.

"A hundred percent, no," Gina admitted. "Of course not. But I'm reasonably certain he won't go there, which is great progress for me. I mean, he's a man, I understand that. Men can be downright dogs, I understand that, too. But I trust my husband one-hundred percent now. I have to. And no, that kind of trust didn't come overnight. Bet that. But it's here now."

"So there's no way under the sun that Dutch can cheat on you, is that what you're telling me?"

"No, I'm not telling you that at all, La. Of course he could cheat! But that's not the question. The question is *will* he cheat? Will he see and not touch? I know he has it in him to touch, but will he touch? I say no."

This surprised LaLa. Gina had never been the type to speak in absolute terms regarding anything, especially what some man who was not in her eyesight twenty-four-seven would or would not do. "And you're absolutely certain of that?" she asked her best friend.

"I'm absolutely certain of my trust in him," Gina answered absolutely. "I would be beyond surprised if Dutch cheated on me. Hell, I'd be a basket case for months."

They both smiled.

"And don't get me wrong," Gina continued. "I'm not sitting up here like some pie-in-the-sky, clueless airhead telling you he never has or never will. I'm telling you I pray daily that he doesn't. There's some serious skanks out there eager to get their hands on my husband, I know that. And his ass is probably just as eager to get his hands on some of them." They both laughed. "But I truly don't believe he'd betray me like that."

"But he's still a man, G."

"I hear you. And you're right. He's still a man. A special man, yes, very special. But he's a man. And you and I both have had our share of heartaches to know that loving a man is a risk no matter who he might be, I feel you, girl. None of them are sure bets."

Although LaLa smiled at that, she was far from comforted. That look of concern returned on her soft, brown-skinned, pretty face. If Dutch Harber wasn't a sure bet, she reasoned, how in the world could Crader ever be? Especially since Crader didn't have half the willpower Dutch seemed to have, and Crader had already cheated on her long before they were married.

But she refused to dwell on all of that. Gina had misgivings about Dutch when they were first married, too. Now she was certain of her man. Or, at least, as certain as you could be about somebody else. But LaLa was going to hold onto that ray of hope. In time, if Crader acted right, she'd be as certain of him, too. She married a gorgeous man, a man who was going to look at the ladies, and the ladies were going to look at him. But she had to trust that he didn't touch. She had to trust that his cheating ways ended forevermore the day he decided to change course, and asked her to marry him.

Crader made his way into the beautifully-appointed Truman Study and plopped down behind the desk.

Allison Shearer, who was standing in front of that desk, waited until he sat down.

"Good afternoon, Mr. Vice President."

"This couldn't wait?"

"No, sir," Allison said and handed him a manila envelope. "It definitely couldn't wait."

Allison slung her long, blonde hair out of her face as Crader slowly opened the envelope and pulled out a newspaper clipping. A yellow post-it note was sticking onto its front. *Show to VP,* the post-it note said.

"Where did you get this?" Crader asked as he removed the post-it note.

"It was mailed to my home."

Crader looked at her. "Your home?" he asked.

"Yes, sir."

Crader looked at the news clipping's headline: *Vegas Couple Killed in Private Plane Crash*. Crader looked down, at the grainy picture of the couple, and then he looked at the names below the picture. Jim and Elvelyn Rosenthal. Didn't ring a bell at all. He looked at Allison.

"What is this about?" he asked, confused.

"I thought you'd be able to tell me," Allison said. "It said for me to show this clipping to you."

Crader looked at the attractive couple again. And then he read the news account. They were on their way to Aspen, Colorado in their private plane, the plane developed engine trouble, and shortly thereafter crashed. They were the only two on board and both were killed. They had been married for a year and a half. They had a child, the guy was a wealthy businessman, both were considered wonderful, vivacious, had everything to live for high society types. Yada, yada, yada.

Crader turned the clipping over, saw nothing, and then looked back at Allison.

"I must be missing something here," he said. "I don't get it."

Allison shrugged her shoulder. "There's certainly something there somebody wanted you to see. I assumed it would be obvious."

But it wasn't. Not to Crader. He looked at the couple again. Jim and Elvelyn Rosenthal. Jim Rosenthal. Nothing. Elvelyn Rosenthal. Nothing. Nothing about this couple was ringing any bells with him whatsoever.

But then, as he stared at the couple, he realized he was staring more at the names than the faces. He looked closely at the faces. And closer still at the woman's face. Elvelyn Rosenthal. Elvelyn. Elvelyn Mitchell? Last time he saw her she had just gotten married. Was never told the man's name and he never asked. Could this be Elvelyn Mitchell? Was this *Elv*?

He looked harder. It was an awful picture for identification purposes. She had on dark shades, a scarf around her neck, and it wasn't a close-up but full-length, and from a distance. But that blonde hair, that tall, thin physique, the way she carried her pocketbook.

His heart began to pound.

"What is it?" Allison asked, her face now as anxious as his appeared.

"Where's Dutch?"

"Crader, what is it?"

"Where's the president?"

"Crader, tell me something!"

"Where's the fucking president!" Crader screamed in his well-known bombastic style, his hand slamming onto his desk. He looked up at Allison. She was offended, but she was also accustomed to Crader's hard edge.

"He's still in Helsinki, at the summit," she reminded him. "He's not due back to the States until late tonight, as soon as the last of those meetings are over. You know his schedule, Cray. Now what is it?"

Crader still sat there, staring at that picture. He knew he had to calm back down. But if it were true . . .

"I need more information," he started mumbling.

"More information about what?" a now worried Allison wanted to know.

But Allison didn't exist right now for Crader. "I need to be certain," he continued to mumble, looking around the room. "I can't just go running to the president half-cock like this, not until I'm certain. But how can I be certain?" he asked with a distressed look on his face. "Who would even send this to me? Who would even know . . ."

And then it hit him like a ton of bricks. He looked up at Allison, although he didn't even notice her there. "Max," he said. "Max Brennan."

"What about Max?" Allison asked.

"Max?" Crader said as if it was a question.

"What about Max?"

"How could Max know . . . He was there twelve years ago, but not. . . Why would he?"

"Why would he what, Crader? What about Max?"

But Crader was already looking away from Allison and at the possibilities that Max Brennan, the president's former chief of staff, a man who'd already betrayed the president's trust royally, could be up to some new shit now. And then, as soon as he thought about Max, he realized the bigger problem. He realized what Elvelyn's death meant. What Jim Rosenthal's death meant.

He rose to his feet so fast that his chair fell backwards.

"Miss Shearer," he said to Allison with a look of undeniable seriousness on his face, "you never received this clipping. Do you understand me?"

Allison frowned. "What is it, Cray?"

"Miss Shearer," Crader said again, clutching the desk, "you never saw this clipping, do you understand me? You don't know anything about this clipping. If you receive any more you are to turn them over to me and me alone. Not my staff. Not your staff. But me and me alone. Without hesitation. Without question. Do I make myself clear?"

Allison was floored. She'd been in Washington long enough to know that when the Vice President of the United States tells you to keep your mouth shut, you had better keep your mouth shut.

Allison was also no fool. Dutch would kick her out on her rear if she didn't do exactly what Crader was ordering her to do right now.

"Yes, sir," she said to the VP. "You've made yourself perfectly clear."

Crader exhaled. He knew he could rely on Ally. "That'll be all," he said to her, attempting to remain upright although he felt like collapsing. Allison could see his distress too, and she knew, in time, she'd be in the loop on just what was going on here. But not now. She left.

Crader sat his chair back up and sunk down into it. He needed more information. He had to know for certain. She could have been blowing smoke up his ass when she came to him last year. This clipping could have nothing to do with that.

Or everything to do with that.

But before he uttered a word of this to Dutch, he had to be certain.

CHAPTER TWO

"It's now or never," Jade said to her mother as they stood in the back of the large reception room in Helsinki, Finland. They watched Dutch Harber meet and greet wealthy Europeans who seemed enthralled with the handsome American president. It was Jade's first time at an event like this with her father, and she marveled at how he knew how to work it. He seemed to just love it, she felt, when she was certain nobody could truly love this.

But he acted as if he was pleased to meet every new face in the reception line. And he enjoyed them with style, too, Jade thought with a smile, as he stood there in his elegant black suit that looked as if it had been stitched onto his tall, muscular body. His wavy black hair was slicked back off of his smooth, tanned forehead, revealing those gorgeous green eyes that were always so sharply focused they looked like glass. He was smiling, shaking every hand, giving successful but otherwise regular people the opportunity to hobnob with the President of the United States. And Jade was once again proud that this man, Walter "Dutch" Harber, was her father.

But she was also restless. Because of her mother. Because she still had to convince her mother that if she wanted Dutch, if she wanted to make him a part of their family and not Gina's, she had to be willing to fight the fight of her life to get him.

Her mother, however, wasn't the kind of woman who understood these things. And it was driving Jade nuts.

"Ma, did you hear me?" Jade said stridently, although she was still staring at her father. "It's now or never. If you don't make up your mind that you're willing to fight for him, you won't get him. You don't know Gina like I know her. She's something else. She won't give him up without a fight."

Samantha "Sam" Redding sipped from her glass of wine and continued to stare her big, almond eyes at Dutch. And on some level she resented him. He swooped into their lives, with all of his power and money and charm, and charmed their daughter away from her. Not to mention how he destroyed Henry Osgood, the only man who could handle Jade, in the process. That boy, whom Sam once had dreams of marrying Jade, was in a wheelchair now, thanks to what Dutch had done to him.

Now she was all alone and their daughter was nothing more than a bitch on two legs that Sam could barely stomach. It was as if Jade left their home in South Carolina and became a drug addict. Only her drug of choice was her own father. And Sam blamed Dutch Harber for this crazy turn their daughter had made. It certainly wasn't her fault. She had Jade under complete control and on the right path, before he came along.

"Ma!" Jade said yet again, this time looking at her mother. Her mother was a black beauty to her, with that dark, velvety smooth skin, that perfect petite body, and brains out of this world. She was, if you asked Jade, the total package. But she wasn't a flirt.

"Ma," Jade said, "are you listening to me?"

"Yes, I'm listening," Sam said. "But once again your air-head has rendered you clueless."

This hurt Jade to her heart, as her mother's sharp tongue always did. But she continued to smile anyway. "I know what I'm talking about," she replied.

"It is a fact that you do not," Sam said caustically. "Because if you did know what you were talking about, you wouldn't be talking about Gina giving up Dutch. It's not about Gina giving up Dutch, that's what you don't seem to grasp. It's never been about that. It's about *Dutch* giving up *Gina*. Will *he* give *her* up, that's the real question. And based on all I've read about that couple, I don't see it. He'll do anything for that woman. You saw him when he went before Congress that time to defend her supposedly good name. Oh, my goodness, that man was so angry it was scary. He loves Gina."

"No, he doesn't!" Jade insisted. "That's what people don't understand. He tolerates Gina. Because she's his wife, and she represents him, he stands by her. But if somebody like you were to get his attention, somebody with brains and who

31

looks way better than Gina on your worse day, he'd dump that bitch like a bad habit. I declare he will, Ma. I know he will! He'll realize why he loved you in the first place and come back to you."

"There was no love in the first place," Sam made clear. "How many times do I have to tell you that? There was no love involved. Just sex. We met in college, had one night of sex, I got pregnant with you and disappeared. End of story."

Only it wasn't the end for Jade. It was just the beginning. Because Dutch Harber belonged to her and her mother. Period. Nobody else. Gina and that question-asking, annoying-ass baby of hers be damned, as far as Jade was concerned.

"He's yours for the taking," Jade finally said. "You just don't realize it."

Sam sipped from her glass of wine and continued to watch Dutch work the room. He certainly would be the grand prize in any contest. That was for damn sure. From his tall, athletic body, to his rakish smile and boyish good looks, she was still kicking herself for not seeing what a prized catch he was all those years ago.

But she was such an oddball then. She didn't want any man in her life, let alone some hunky rich white boy like Dutch Harber. But she was so much older now, and wiser, and, if truth be told, much lonelier. So much lonelier. When she was young, being alone was a badge of honor to her. She loved being all by herself. Now it just reminded her of all she didn't have.

But what Jade was talking about, with all of the game-playing and seductive tricks, she wasn't feeling, either. Because she knew what it took to get Dutch Harber, and it wasn't going to involve playing games. He was too smart for that. Her best chance of having him again, not to mention his untold millions of dollars that she desperately needed, was to know his weakness. He was a softie when it came to Jade. All of those years where he wasn't a part of Jade's life, the guilt of it, necessitated that. Therefore, to get him back, all she felt she had to do was to keep Jade under her thumb. Which, even dumb Jade didn't realize, was exactly what she planned to do. It was exactly why she came to Helsinki to begin with.

"I just don't see it," she said to her insistent daughter. "Why would he suddenly leave his wife and young son for me?"

"Because he loves you. I just feel it in my heart. And because Regina Harber doesn't tolerate fools easily and she won't allow any accusation to go unanswered. She's a fighter, Ma. But she's a street fighter. She doesn't know how to finesse it. She always gets embroiled in some scandal or another, I mean all the time. The woman can't help herself. But this will be different. It'll go directly to her character. And Daddy will finally see her for what she really is and drop her so fast you'll get whiplash just watching her fall."

"Oh, please," Sam said, unconvinced. "They tried all that shit before. Dutch isn't going to fall for any of that bash Gina nonsense. He's not going to believe that his wife is some drug addicted sex pervert who sneak men into the White House and---"

"And that's not what I'm talking about, thank-you very much," Jade pointed out. "I know he won't go for that. She won't be sneaking anybody anywhere. This will be done in broad daylight. That's the beauty of it. No sneaking at all. In fact," Jade said with a wry smile, "she won't even realize she's destroying herself until she's destroyed. That's the beauty of it, Ma. I did my homework on that sister. I know exactly how to push her buttons."

"Oh, yeah, Miss Brilliant with the average IQ. How do you push her buttons, please tell me that?"

Jade hesitated. She despised her mother's constant put-down of her intellect. No, she didn't have the kind of pliable, brilliant mind her mother had. But she was no idiot either.

"Well?" Sam asked. "How do you push these buttons of Gina's?"

Jade smiled, remembering to not take any of her mother's constant putdowns personally. Sam was Sam and would always be odd that way. She learned to live with that sad fact a long time ago. "I'll push her buttons one brother at a time," she said.

Sam, who was known for her keen intellect, stared at her daughter. "Marcus Rance?" she asked. "This scheme of yours involves her brother Marcus Rance?"

Jade was impressed. "You're quick," she said. "Yes, Ma. He'll be working with us."

"But why would he want to do anything that could hurt his own half-sister? What are you talking about? Gina was the one who busted her butt to get him out of prison."

"Daddy got him out of prison, not her!" Jade said this angrily. She hated when Gina got credit for anything. "Daddy got him out! He was the one who got that governor to pardon him or whatever they did for him. It wasn't Gina!"

"All right," Sam said. "It wasn't Gina, I get it. Damn. You just need to calm yourself back down before you make yourself look more foolish than you already look."

Jade did manage to calm down. She even smiled her beautiful, bright white smile. "Marcus has been staying with me and Christian. Gina wouldn't let him stay at the White House, you know."

"That's not what I heard. I heard Dutch kicked him out."

"Because Gina made him," Jade insisted.

Sam looked at her daughter with amazement in her eyes. If Jade believed for a second that anybody *made* Dutch Harber do anything he didn't want to do, she was more ignorant than Sam had given her credit for.

"Marcus has been great," Jade went on. "He was really there for me after my. . . after what happened with my baby."

"After your miscarriage, Jade," Sam said pointblank. "Not after what happened to the baby. After your miscarriage. Call it what it is."

"Ma, okay," Jade said irritably. And then calmed down again. Tried to shield her true emotions again. "All I'm saying is that I can talk to Marcus. He gets what I'm about better than anybody else ever could. And guess what, Ma? Marcus agrees with me. He can't stand Gina, either. He feels she visited him in prison, not to help him, but because it wouldn't look right for the First Lady to ignore her own brother. She doesn't care anything about him. She doesn't even have time for him and just tossed him off on me and Christian. But he'll do anything for me, Ma. And I mean anything," Jade added with a cunning grin and sipped her wine.

Sam stared at her daughter. Was about to go there with her daughter. But Christian Bale, Jade's husband, came over.

"The President's almost wrapping it up, ladies," he informed them with that usual cheerful lilt in his voice. "He's going to be so happy to see you, Miss Redding."

Jade rolled her eyes. "Do call her Sam or mother-in-law or something less formal, Christian, my goodness. Don't call her *Miss Redding*. She's not that old yet."

Christian blushed red. Sometimes Jade took him on such wild rides when he didn't even know they were going anywhere. "I didn't mean to imply that she was old. I was just---"

"It's okay, Christian," Sam said. "Don't pay Jade and her foolishness any attention."

Christian, however, couldn't help but pay her attention. She was his wife. And he loved her. "She's okay," he said to his mother-in-law.

Sam stared at him. He was in his mid-twenties, but looked even younger. His blond hair was stacked high on his round head, and his blue eyes were big and milky. And this kid was supposed to tame Jade? Sam wanted to laugh at such a ludicrous proposition.

"You really ought to sit down," Christian suggested to his wife. "The doctor said you shouldn't overexert yourself."

Jade, however, would have none of it. "How is standing up an overexertion, Christian, will you tell me that, please?"

"The doctor said you shouldn't overdo it."

"He said that two weeks ago. I had a bad cold, Christian, that's all. That's over and done with. I can do backflips now as far as that doctor is concerned. Geez."

Christian didn't argue with her. The president had already told him that loving a woman like Jade wasn't going to be a cakewalk. Christian understood that. But that didn't make it any easier.

A tall young man with a buzz cut approached the threesome. "Excuse me, Miss Redding, but the president will see you now."

"Thanks, Rick," Christian said to the young man, and the young man nodded at Christian.

"Right this way, ma'am," the young man said, and Sam began to follow him. Jade, however, began to follow them. But Christian pulled her back.

"Maybe your mom should speak to the president alone," he suggested.

Jade, however, looked at him as if he was crazy. Because she just knew he was out of his natural mind if he though she wasn't going to include herself in this meeting. She broke away from his grasp, and followed her mother.

They walked into a private room, off from the reception area, where Dutch was standing alone. He was looking out of the window, his hands in his pants pockets, his back to the entrance.

"Miss Redding is here, Mr. President," young Rick said, bowed, and left.

Sam and Jade stood before Dutch. When he turned around, and saw Sam in her form-fitting, sequined dress, a kind of aqua-blue that highlighted her beautiful eyes and dark, velvety-smooth skin, his throat caught. She'd always been a looker, he thought. But right now she was simply stunning.

She smiled when he turned around. "Hello, Rookie," she said in that deadpan way of hers that made Dutch snort. Rookie was her nickname for him when they were both students at Harvard.

He went to her.

There was a momentary awkwardness, where neither knew quite what to do, but then Dutch reached over and gave her a hug. Sam closed her eyes when he touched her, but fought hard not to show her feelings.

Dutch wasn't quite so successful in shielding his. She not only looked great, he thought has he hugged her, she smelled great, too. And as they began to part he gave her a peck on the cheek.

"You look fabulous," he said to her, admiring her fine physique. Jade smiled at the way Dutch perused her mother's body.

"Thank-you," Sam said. She was unaccustomed to compliments, and still didn't quite know how to accept them.

"Would you care for something to drink?"

"You too," Sam said.

There was a slight hesitation, as Dutch wasn't sure if he missed something. "Pardon me?" he asked her.

"No, I was, I was going to say that you look wonderful too. Or fabulous as the actual term was. You too, that's what I was saying in reference to what you had said about me. That I looked fabulous. I was . . . ."

Jade rolled her eyes. Her mother really was a band of one.

"Well, thank-you, Sam," Dutch said, not at all taken aback by her differentness. "Would you care for something to drink?"

"No, no, I'm good. I'm fine."

Dutch offered her a seat, and he sat down in the flanking chair. Jade sat on the arm of the chair, beside her father. Dutch crossed his legs, staring at Sam. Sam crossed her legs, staring at him.

"So," Dutch said, unbuttoning his suit coat, "our daughter here says you wanted to see me."

"Yes. Yes, I did." He seemed to become more attractive with age, Sam thought, as she sat there. And the way it felt to be in his arms. She felt so safe there. The idea that she let a guy like this get away from her when he was obviously infatuated with her all those years ago made her angry with herself. But she was such a different person then.

Dutch waited for her to tell him why she wanted to see him. When she didn't say anything, Jade did.

"Go on and tell him," she said.

Sam exhaled. "I wanted to let you know that I was thinking about staying, that is, Jade and Christian have offered to let me stay with them in Washington for a little while. Until I can work some things out." Sam said this and stared at Dutch, to gauge his reaction. Dutch didn't immediately respond.

Jade, surprised by this, looked at him.

"I wanted to know how you felt about that," Sam said.

"I don't think it's a good idea," Dutch said honestly.

Jade was surprised by his reaction. "Why wouldn't it be a good idea, Daddy?"

"I think you and Christian have issues you're trying to work out and I don't think a third party living in your home is a good idea right now. I feel the same way about Marcus being there. But it's not my decision to make."

"But it matters what you think, Dutch," Sam said. "Very much."

"But we want her to stay with us," Jade said in that sometimes bratty way of hers Dutch didn't like. "It's just until she work some things out."

"As I said," Dutch reiterated, "it's not my decision."

"But she's my mother. She's having hard times. Why wouldn't you want my mother to spend a little time with me?"

Dutch looked at Sam. "What hard times?" he asked her.

Sam looked away from him. He had already concluded that she didn't come all this way to Finland just to ask if he approved of her staying with Jade for a while. There was more to this tale. A lot more, he determined. He also determined that Sam was the kind of prideful person who wouldn't want to discuss any "hard times" in front of her daughter.

He looked at their daughter. "Why don't you go see what Chris is up to," he said to her. "I want to speak privately with your mother."

Jade, however, was still perturbed with Dutch. "Why can't Ma stay with me? What's wrong with that?"

"We'll talk about it later."

"But I want her with me. She's my mother. She wouldn't be any burden on me."

Dutch gave his daughter a look that could chill the sun. A look Jade knew all too well. She didn't like doing so, she hated it, in fact. But that look told her not to push it. She therefore got up, and left the room.

Sam shook her head. "She's a grown woman," she said with a smile, "but in age only."

Dutch, however, didn't return the smile. His issues with Jade weren't funny to him. "Why did you want to see me, Samantha?" he asked her. "You didn't come all this way about any living arrangements."

Sam exhaled, uncrossed her legs, leaned back, and crossed them again. Dutch looked down at those shapely legs. He realized, to his own surprise, that he was getting aroused as he looked at her.

"You're correct," Sam finally said. "I most definitely didn't come here about living arrangements."

Dutch waited for her to continue. She didn't. "Why did you come?" he asked her.

She let out a frustrated exhale. "It's been a tough few years. I can't lie." She looked at him. "A really tough few years."

"For the bookstore?"

"The bookstore, me, everything. The truth of the matter is, I'm broke, Dutch. I'm nearing bankruptcy. It's been tough."

Dutch stared at her. He had not expected this. "How much?" he asked.

Sam paused. "The bookstore is the worst of it. It's swimming in a sea of red. I mortgaged the house twice to staunch some of the bleeding. Now I'm about to lose both of them."

"House and bookstore?"

"Right."

How much debt are we talking, Sam?"

"A couple hundred thousand," she said. "For starters." Then tears began to appear in her pretty eyes. "I'm sorry," she said, wiping them away.

"Nothing to be sorry about. It's a rough economy for everybody. I know that."

"I thought I could make that bookstore work. I tried everything. Buy one, get one free, reading labs, book signings, but nothing worked. Some days a handful of people come through, other days nobody walks through that door." She wiped more tears away.

"It's okay, Sam," Dutch said as he uncrossed his legs and leaned forward. "Don't beat yourself up."

"I never learned how to do it, Dutch," she admitted, her almond eyes looking at him with a questioning glare. "I thought I had it figured out, but I never learned how to do it. I did what my parents had wanted and earned my medical degree. That was a big deal. I was as proud as they were. But then I tossed that aside to go into the bookstore business. Something I thought I would love. Now I can't even do that right." She covered her mouth as the tears returned. Dutch quickly left his seat and moved over to her. He sat beside her and pulled her into his arms.

"It's okay," he said, holding her.

It felt heady for her to feel his arms around her again. But she thought about her condition, about what sorry state her life was in, and the tears returned.

"I thought I had it all figured out," she said again. "Now I'm so broke I have to move in with my own daughter."

"Sam, it's okay," Dutch said as her sobbing increased.

"I'll have to try and get a job at a hospital, to help pay off the creditors, but there's no guarantee they'll hold off that long." She shook her head. "How could I get myself in this position? I feel like such a failure!"

The idea of a strong woman like Sam this beaten down shook Dutch too. And he pulled her closer. "It's okay."

"I should have gotten out when I realized it wasn't working. But I was so stubborn. I was going to make it work. No matter what. Now look at me."

"Sam, it's okay. I'll take care of it. All of it. Don't worry."

Sam at first was sure she didn't hear him right. He'd take care of all of it? The most she had hoped for was a small loan to keep her largest creditors temporarily at bay, until she could get back on her feet.

She looked at him. "I can't ask you---"

"You aren't asking me. I'm telling you that I'll take care of it."

Sam stared at Dutch. She once had a chance with him. And they were equals then.

"Thank-you," she said, and moved back into his arms.

Yes, she thought, as she closed her eyes. She didn't have to play any seduction games whatsoever. All she had to do was keep Jade close at hand, keep little Jade under her thumb, and Dutch would automatically follow.

CHAPTER THREE

Dutch stepped out of the helicopter, saluted the Marine on duty, and made his way in a lumbering gait across the south lawn of the White House. It was nearly one in the morning, he was dead on his feet, and he felt, in an odd way, very lonely. Jade and Christian left Helsinki after the reception yesterday, taking a relieved Sam with them, but he was forced to stay and attend more emergency meetings that netted a big fat zero in terms of results. Which meant the media was going to have a field day with his lack of success. Europe's economic woes were of their own making, but the American press was sure to blame their American president. Now he was back in DC, back at the White House, and missing Gina terribly.

As he made his way through the doors of the South Portico, saluting the Marine guarding the door, he knew Gina would be fast asleep this time of morning. She always tried to hang, he thought amusingly as he walked along the corridor, but she never could. Not that it mattered. He missed her so much he knew he was going to wake her up regardless.

He made his way upstairs to the quiet Residence, stopping in the Nursery first to eyeball a sleeping Little Walt. The Nanny on duty stood to her feet, but Dutch motioned her back down. Then he reached over the bed and kissed his young son on the forehead. Walt seemed to smile unconsciously at just the smell of his father's nearness. It warmed Dutch's heart just watching his reaction. Then he kissed him on the forehead again, and headed for the presidential suite.

He was right: Gina was fast asleep. But she was lying across the bed in clothes, a short skirt and a belly-button length blouse, as if she had tried with all she had to stay awake for his arrival. He just stood there, his hands in his pants pockets, his expensive suit now rumpled, watching her. He had a serious physical reaction to her, that was certain. His cock was rock hard within seconds of seeing her tight ass on that bed. He, in fact, wanted to fuck her so badly he could taste it.

But he had an emotional reaction to her as well. He loved her. He loved everything about Regina Harber. The press was going to call him a loser for not being able to negotiate some compromise on European debt, and the Congress was going to pile on, too. They would make the repeated point that if Europe's economy falls, the U.S. would be next. But Gina would be in his corner. She always was. And that, for Dutch, was priceless. It was why he got out of bed every day. It was why he did all he could to remain faithful to her.

He had planned to shower on Air Force One on the trip back to the States, so that he could hit that thang of Gina's as soon as he hit the sheets, but he was so tired he had fallen asleep on the plane.

He therefore went to the adjacent bathroom, undressed quickly, and jumped into the shower. He thought about many things as he cleansed his aching muscles. He thought about Jade and that devil-may-care side of her that was beginning to alarm him. He would talk to Gina, to see what she thought, but he was beginning to lean toward therapy for that young woman. Before she did some real harm, he thought.

And he thought about Jade's mother. Her oddness had undoubtedly made her a lousy parent, and now Jade, unfortunately, bore the burdens of that lousiness. But how could he judge Sam? He wasn't there to help rear the child. He wasn't there to temper Sam's toughness and sensibleness with the emotional attachment a child also needed. Sam had no intentions of ever being anybody's mother. She and he both knew she wasn't cut out for anything like that. But Dutch kept hounding her for sex. Every time he saw her he was trying to get her in his bed. And in a moment of weakness, she caved.

At first they wore protection. Wore it the second time, too. But by the third round in that wild night of sex, they didn't care. They fucked raw. Fucked like rabbits in the raw. And the result of that momentary lapse would last their lifetimes.

Dutch still wondered what Jade's youth had been like. His now deceased mother had threatened to have her friends in high places make Sam's life a living hell if she carried the baby to term. She therefore told Dutch that she had had an abortion, and then disappeared from sight. He didn't know Jade even existed until she was twenty-three years old. Old enough to have Sam's brand of rearing deep within her. Old enough to be, in some ways, even odder than her mother.

And Sam was definitely odd. She still wore it like a second skin. She was still that tough-as-nails, do it her way Sam. Still had that toughness down pat. But now she needed help, she said to him, which he knew was a hard admission for her to make. Which made Dutch admire her even more. Not that she was this great, empathetic person worthy of any admiration. She wasn't a particularly likeable human being, if he was to tell the truth of it.

But he admired her because she was always true to herself. That took courage and it took conviction, and Sam, for all her faults, had both in spades. And a woman like that, who raised their daughter alone, who went through med school on scholarships alone, who gave up a lucrative practice to fulfill her dream of owning a bookstore, now considered herself a failure. A failure. A woman with her brains and beauty and talents.

Dutch would gladly help a woman like that. He was a very wealthy man. He would not hesitate in helping a self-reliant, honest soul like Sam. She had planned to return to her medical career, only because she needed the money, but Dutch had told her to not make any rash decisions just yet. He knew she really wanted to keep her bookstore. That was her true love. He, in fact, already had his lawyers looking into the feasibility of such a proposition, and until they reported back to him, he told her to wait. And Sam, to his pleasant surprise, was finally willing to take direction from somebody else. A part of him was very pleased that he was the one to whom she was willing to relinquish some control.

But why was he so pleased? That was the real question. When they were kids in college he used to have such a crush on Sam, an unbelievable crush, and seeing her look so stunning in that sequined dress yesterday turned him on mightily. But he couldn't possibly still be harboring any feelings in that department. Not with a woman like Gina waiting this very moment in his bed. Sam was fine, and was perhaps a woman with the greatest natural beauty he'd ever seen, but she was no Gina.

He, in fact, was getting hard again just thinking about Gina. And what, he knew, he was about to do to her.

He stepped out of the shower, dried off quickly, and tossed the white towel onto the elongated, marbled vanity.

As soon as he walked back into the bedroom, Gina was just beginning to stir awake. He smiled. Because as soon as her big, golden-brown eyes opened, and she saw him standing there naked as the night was long, she made him understand why he loved her so much.

"*Dutch*!" she screamed so heartfelt, as if she had been on a deserted island and he was her water. She jumped from the bed and ran to him. His heart was hammering with joy as he lifted her up into his arms. It had been almost a week that they'd been apart, but it felt like a year.

"Oh, my darling!" he said as he twirled her around happily. And then they both found each other's mouth, and all sounds stopped. Except the sound of their smacking, and tongue kissing, and making up for lost time with their lips alone.

Dutch was moaning as he kissed Gina. He moaned so hard that she almost smiled. By the way he was going at it she would have declared they'd been parted for a very long time. Not that she wasn't going at it too. She was. And almost as hard as he was. She wrapped her legs around his rock hard body and her arms around his neck, and relaxed into his kiss.

Dutch relaxed too, in the warmth of having Gina in his arms again. It felt positively exhilarating to feel her body wrapped around his, his dick jammed against her mound, and her lips on his lips. And her ass. His hands reached beneath her skirt, beneath her panties, and began massaging her ass.

Until his moaning became a grunt, and he knew he had to find more relief.

He carried her to their bed, still kissing her, still massaging her, and sat her on the bed. As he began removing her shirt, Gina took his fully aroused dick in her hand. She began licking it, slowly up and down and around, in that half-gliding, taste-so-good way Dutch just adored.

"Oh, babe," he said as she licked around his head, "that mouth of yours is a lethal weapon!"

"Only for you," Gina said as she licked up and down and squeezed as she licked.

Dutch leaned down too, and began fondling her breasts, as he felt the wonderment of Gina's tongue all over his rod. Her breasts were full now, her nipples hard, and he couldn't stop twirling and squeezing them. But the more Gina licked on him, the less he was able to do to her. And soon he couldn't do anything but stand there completely paralyzed by her slick administrations. It felt so good to him that it made his entire body tremble in waves of sensation.

And Gina kept at it. Her tongue felt every vein in his rod, as it continued to stretch long and expand wide. And to throb. She licked the top tip of his head, right in the seam, as it began a slow leak.

But when she went down on Dutch, all the way down, he thought he was going to cum in her mouth. But he didn't. He held back. Because he had to do her first. No-way was it ending this quickly.

He leaned down and lifted her slightly. He removed her skirt and panties, rendering her naked too.

Then he knelt down, placed her legs over his shoulders, and opened her wide. He loved the look of her pink pussy. Loved the smell of her. He'd missed it. They rarely went this long without his mouth, his dick, all over it. And he didn't linger long. He placed his mouth between those legs, into that pussy, and licked.

Gina felt a surge of electricity slink through her when Dutch's tongue first touched her folds. She rested on her hands, palm down, behind her, and her head leaned back too. It was as if she was giving herself completely to him, and he was poised to take it.

His big hands slid underneath her butt and squeezed as he ate her. All she could hear was his smacking sounds as his mouth met her moistness and delivered a powerful blow to her cunt. She hadn't felt his tongue in days, now she wanted him to devour her.

And he did. He pulled her so close that her ass was nearly off of the bed's edge, and his face buried itself like a wedge between her legs. It felt strangely awesome to have the leader of the free world on his knees giving her this kind of head, and she enjoyed every second of that awesomeness. And when his finger entered her vagina to compliment his tongue, and they slid in and out of her as if they were in unison, she fell back onto the bed. Her back arched as the intensity built, as his fingers fucked her, as his tongue fucked her. Until it was more than she could bear.

"Dutch, no," she let out, her breath now raspy and hoarse.

"Yes, Gina," Dutch said breathlessly. His mouth and fingers were now whipping into her, working her over as if she was the meal of his life.

"No, Dutch, no!" she yelled again. She arched again. "I can't take it!"

But she knew she wanted to. Desperately. Because as soon as he stopped and looked up at her, to make sure she truly wanted him to stop, she quickly changed her tune.

"No," she yelled. "Don't stop!"

Dutch smiled, although his lustful look shielded it. And he was at it again.

He moved his free hand to his cock, and began jerking on it, as the feeling of Gina's wetness sliding around his tongue caused him to throb almost to the point of no return. He had to have it. He had to have it NOW.

He slid her further up onto the bed, got on the bed with her, and opened her legs as wide as they could go. With his knees between those legs, he pulled her closer, until her legs were across his thighs. He then slid his dick into her folds with the deftness of a man seeking refuge. Both of them let out a sigh of welcome when he entered her. It felt like a tease, where the anticipation was so great it couldn't possibly live up to the hype.

Only it did live up to it, they realized, as soon as Dutch moved in deeper. It surpassed all expectations.

"*Ah, Dutch*," Gina cried and arched and kept crying the further he dug in. And he dug in. He was showing no mercy. He kept digging in. He laid down on her, digging in. He lifted her ass, squeezing her, and digging in.

He gave her the best he had to give, as his thick dick stroked inside of her with expert strokes and then started sliding against her walls. His dick came alive in her pussy. His slide and strokes felt so intense and sensual that she kept squeezing his massive biceps, attempting to ease that wonderful intensity she really didn't want eased, and then she started screaming his name. She screamed the sounds of unbridled joy he loved to hear from her. Because he knew, when Gina screamed, he was pleasing her beyond measure.

He kept pleasing her, long and hard, all of the disappointment of Helsinki and the press criticisms and DC politics disappearing into thin air as he felt his wife's pussy come to life around his cock. And it latched onto him like an attachment, and wouldn't let him move without friction.

He loved her friction. It made his pathway narrow and sweet. And all he wanted to do was lay there and fuck her. He banged her. He pumped her. He pounded her. Gina was feeling every thrash to the roots of her hair. She even squeezed his ass, and was holding on for wonderful dear life, as he thrashed her.

He held her tightly in his arms as he fucked her. "Oh, *Gina*," he started saying, as the feelings intensified to even heights he hadn't anticipated. "*Gina*!" he said again, his hands coursing through her soft, short hair, his mouth kissing her all over her pretty face. "*Gina*!"

And his dick kept thrashing against her walls every time he said her name. He slid, in and almost out, in and almost out, his dick filling up with her love. And the sounds in the silence was deafening. The bed creaking. The grunts and groans. And the slushing sounds of her saturation and his movements inside that saturation caused them both to fall into a rhythm that became a song. And Dutch, Gina felt, sung it better than any man had ever attempted to sing it before.

Dutch then moved onto his back, taking Gina with him. Now she was on top of him. But nothing changed. He was still inside of her. He was still pounding her with a fierceness they could barely take. Gina laid down on his thick chest, her love for him becoming like a drug. And when he wrapped his arms around her, melding her to him, making her *his* again, she wanted to cry.

She'd never had a man like Dutch before. She'd never felt the kind of love he gave to her before, and the respect. He took care of her. In the bedroom and all points in between. And as his dick side-swiped her pussy, and as he fucked her with an aggression that made it clear who was in charge of this union, she closed her eyes in deep down satisfaction. And she let him stay in charge.

Dutch could feel her heartbeat as he fucked her. He could feel her body shivering and arching and stretching against his body. He rubbed her ass, and squeezed her ass, as his cock kept giving her a glide. He missed this. He missed her. He wanted to leave a streak inside of her from his pounding alone. He wanted to leave his mark.

And that was when it happened. That was when they came. Gina arched and he tightened and they came. It felt like a grunted-out exhale. It felt like a pouring out of love. And when they couldn't bear it anymore, it felt like an explosion.

Dutch grabbed her and held her and met her body arch with an arch of his own. He wanted to spill out deep inside of her. He wanted to leave her scorched with his love. And she was scorched. By the time he finished putting that pounding on her, she felt as if she was on fire with his love.

When they stopped shaking with the drain of sexual satisfaction, and were able to move at all, Dutch managed to pull out of Gina. It immediately reignited that sensual friction his deep penetration created, but he still managed to move. He got out of bed.

He went into the bathroom, peed and cleansed his penis, and then returned with a damp cloth. Gina knew the routine. Dutch did this often.

She therefore moved higher on the pillows, as he opened her legs.

"Enjoyed it?" he asked as he sat there, legs crossed, and wiped her.

Gina looked at this gorgeous man, as his silky black hair dropped cross his forehead. She smiled. "What do you think?"

"I don't mean to brag," Dutch said, playfully bragging, "but I think you had the time of your life, kid."

Gina laughed and swatted the powerful biceps of his muscular arms. "Don't flatter yourself, Mister," she said, causing Dutch to laugh too.

When he finished cleaning her, he kissed her on her lower lips. Gina even closed her eyes momentarily as a tingle slinked through her vagina when he kissed her there. And then she smiled and shook her head. When it came to Dutch's touch, she was through dealing.

Dutch went back into the bathroom to discard the cloth. When he returned he lifted Gina into his arms, pulled back the covers, and put them both to bed.

He pulled Gina into his arms and just held her there. They were face to face, and he kissed her nose.

"What have I missed while I was gone?" he asked, looking at her hair and running his fingers through it.

"Not much," Gina said after little thought. "I'm volunteering now over at a community center and Marcus is helping me."

"Really?"

"He's surprisingly good at it, too. The people love him. They see him as one of them. They see me as the president's wife."

Dutch smiled. "Good. Because that's exactly what you are. You're mine."

"I'm also Gina from the block. As in Block by Block Raiders? Remember BBR? Hell, I used to work with gang bangers, drug dealers, prostitutes, you name it. The good people from that center would cringe if they knew the clientele I used to serve. Now all they see is this dainty little First Lady. Dutch Harber's wife."

Dutch stared at her. He always suspected that being his wife had taken a toll on Gina. "Do you ever feel as though you've lost something of yourself since being married to me?"

"Being married to you, Dutch Harber, no. Being married to Walter Dutch Harber, the President of the United States, yes. Of course. I'm walking in your shadow right now. And you cast a mighty big shadow." Gina smiled. Dutch just continued to stare at her. "It's temporary. That's why I've been thinking."

Dutch lifted on one elbow, the side of his face resting on his fist. "Go on," he said.

"When you're no longer president, and we're private citizens again, have you thought about a place for us to live?"

"I told you about those properties I own across the globe."

"Yes, I know about those. And they all sound brilliant. But . . ."

"I also know," Dutch continued slowly, "that I'm a product of Nantucket, but you're a Newark kind of gal."

Gina smiled. "Right," she said, amazed that he realized where she was going with this. She continued to stare at him, praying he would take it to the conclusion she was hoping for.

"That's why," he went on, slowly, "I thought we might start looking at some properties in the Newark area. To have a home there."

"Oh, Dutch!" Gina said as she lunged into his arms. He pulled her over, on top of him. "You don't mind?"

Dutch began running his fingers through Gina's hair again. He loved the feel of her scalp. He loved her hair short and bouncy. "Why would I mind?" he asked her.

"Because," Gina said as if it was obvious, "Newark is great, it's a wonderful place, but it's no Nantucket or Kennebunkport or any of those ritzy kind of places."

Dutch laughed. He began rubbing her ass. "Understood."

"But you'll be willing to live there, to make a city that still has its share of issues your main home?"

"Absolutely. It's your home. You love Newark. I never even liked Nantucket."

"Really?"

"Really. I was born and raised on that Island, lived the good life there, but it never felt like home to me. I've never felt at home anywhere, to tell you the truth, not even here in DC, until you became a part of my life here. So why would I want to go back to Nantucket? No. Newark is your home, you love the place, so it's going to become me and Walt's home too."

Gina stared at him with that sincere look he loved. "Thank-you," she said heartfelt.

"I'll get our attorneys to quietly arrange for a realtor to begin coordinating potential properties there. We may have to have something built."

"That'll be fine by me," Gina said, getting excited by the possibilities. "I truly cannot wait until your term in office is over. Our real life will begin then."

Dutch smiled. "Oh, so this life we're living now is just what? The dress rehearsal?"

"Exactly that," Gina said with a smile of her own. "When we get to Newark, me, you, and Little Walt, we are going to set that town on fire!"

Dutch laughed. Then the telephone began ringing. Gina looked at the nightstand.

"If it's not the Red Phone," Dutch said half joking, "we're not home."

Gina, however, was concerned. It was after two in the morning and was their direct line. She answered the phone. "Hello?"

"Let me speak to my daddy," Jade's voice bellowed out.

Gina was, at first, taken aback by her rudeness. Not that she was surprised by it. She wasn't. That therapist Dutch had forced her to go and see last year had told her that she would be Jade's natural enemy. Not for anything Gina would ever do to Jade. But because of Gina's position in Dutch's life. Jade didn't know her father while she was growing up. Now she was overcompensating for his affections.

But it was three o'clock in the morning. Even affection-starved Jade wouldn't phone this time of morning unless something serious had happened. Gina handed the phone to Dutch.

"Who?" he asked before he would take it.

"Your daughter," Gina said.

Dutch was still peeved by the interruption, but he answered the phone. "What is it, Jade?" he asked her.

"Daddy, you've got to come over!" Jade insisted.

"And why do I need to do that?"

"It's mom."

"Sam?" he said, now concerned. Gina looked at him.

"Yes!" Jade said. "She's acting so weird! She's screaming and seeing people that's not there and I don't know what to do! You've got to come!"

Dutch's heart began to pound. "I'm on my way," he said, Jade voiced her appreciation, and then he hung up the phone.

"What's the matter?" Gina asked as she moved off of him. He began to get out of bed.

"It's Sam," he said. "Jade says she's behaving strangely."

Gina frowned. "But Sam's in South Carolina. How would Jade know how she's behaving?"

"She's here," Dutch said as he headed for the walk-in closet, his tight ass making Gina long to squeeze it again. "She's staying with Jade and Chris for a little while."

"Really?" Gina asked, astounded. She was sitting up in bed now. "Since when?"

"She came to see me in Finland," Dutch said from the closet, as he grabbed a pair of jeans off of the hangar and began to put them on.

"Finland?" Gina was saying. "Sam was in Helsinki with you?"

It was only then did Dutch realize his error. He hadn't mentioned Sam to Gina. He peered out of the closet and looked at her. "She came yesterday. She needed to talk to me."

This sounded incredulous to Gina. "So instead of waiting for you to come back to the States, she decides to hop a plane to Finland just to talk to you?"

"Probably more Jade's decision than hers, but yes." Then he stared at Gina. "Come slip on some clothes," he said. "I want you to come with me."

Gina wasn't at all sure if she wanted to come with him, but she got out of bed anyway. Gina always inwardly felt that if anyone had the capacity to steal Dutch away from her, it would be Samantha Redding. She was odd as hell, sometimes off-the-chain odd. What woman, Gina often wondered, would give up a lucrative medical practice to open a struggling bookstore? And the way she was so gun-ho about Henry Osgood's relationship with Jade when she knew that man was emotionally abusing her daughter, made her just plain weird in Gina's book.

But Dutch still had a soft spot for Sam. She raised their daughter alone, being threatened by Dutch's powerful mother to get rid of the child. Sam didn't get rid of the unborn child, but she told Dutch that she had had an abortion. When he found out the truth some twenty-three years after that lie was told to him, he never recovered from it. He didn't blame Sam. She was fighting for her life against forces she was rightly fearful of. He blamed his now deceased mother. And, it seemed to Gina, he felt as responsible for Sam as he did for Jade.

Gina began putting on her clothes. Sam Redding. She was worrisome to her on many levels. And it had nothing to do with her gorgeousness, although she was drop-dead gorgeous. But she mainly worried Gina because, of all the other women Dutch had ever had in his life, only Sam, like Gina, shared that bond of procreation with him. Only Sam, like Gina, could carry that special mantle of being Dutch Harber's baby mama.

CHAPTER FOUR

Christian, Jade, and Marcus were in the living room by the time the dark SUV pulled into the home's garage and Dutch and Gina, under full Secret Service protection, stepped out. The door leading into the home from the garage was designated as the Secret Service entrance and was never to be locked, was opened by an agent and Dutch and Gina entered the mud room that led into the home's living area.

As soon as they entered the living area, Jade broke away from the two men and ran to her father. Dutch pulled her into his arms.

"Thanks so much for coming," she said to him.

"You okay?" he asked her, rubbing her hair.

Jade nodded her head. "I'm better now that you're here," she said. She glanced at Gina, who, like her father, was dressed in jeans and a jersey. "Oh, hello," she said to Gina, putting on a smile. "I didn't think you'd come too." Jade, in fact, was counting on Gina *not* coming.

Gina figured as much by her reaction. "Yes, I came," Gina said, refusing to play any games with anyone this time of morning.

Dutch had his arm around Jade's waist, but he was extending his hand. "Hello, Chris, Marcus," he said as the two men approached and they shook his hand.

Marcus and Dutch didn't get along, but you wouldn't know it by looking at them. They themselves never so much as mentioned it, and were always cordial toward the other. But Dutch had taken the measure of the man after he helped to get him released from that Texas prison. And he didn't like what he saw. Gina was angry with him, but he made it clear that Marcus could not stay at the White House with his wife and son.

Marcus, of course, insisted that Dutch was prejudiced against him. He believed that it was because of his background as a reformed drug dealer and the fact that he had been in prison for murder, even though he was wrongfully accused, that had Dutch so put-off by him. He was reformed, and had cleaned up his act years ago, but Dutch seemed unconvinced.

But for Dutch it went far deeper than that. He believed in redemption as well as any man. It wasn't a question of that. But he was taking no chances with his wife and young son. Gina didn't know Marcus Rance to be offering up any character assurances. She'd only seen him a few times in her entire life by the time he was released from prison. No way was Dutch allowing this virtual stranger, a stranger who may or may not be reformed, to stay under the same roof as his wife and child. Especially as often as he was out of town. He even protested Marcus staying with Jade and Christian. But they were grown and they insisted. They, in fact, moved him right into their DC home despite

Dutch's verbalized misgivings.   And now, against Dutch's advice, they had Sam with them, too.

"Hello, sir," Christian said.   "Hello, Mrs. Harber."

"Hi, Christian," Gina said with a smile.   "Hey, Mark."

"What's up?" Marcus said.   Although he faulted both of them for kicking him out of the White House and making him feel like tossed-out garbage, he knew he had to stay on good terms with his sister.   When it all came down to where the rubber meets the road, Gina, even he understood, was all he had.

"Where's Samantha?" Dutch asked.

"In the bedroom," Jade said.   "It was scary, Daddy."

"She's still in a state?" he asked.   Christian knew she was never really in any state to begin with, but he didn't know how to say it without setting Jade off.

"It was so scary," Jade said again.

Dutch kissed her on the forehead.   "I'll be back," he said as he headed down the hall.   Jade immediately moved to follow him, but Christian grabbed her arm.   "Let your Dad handle it," he said.

"It's my mother, Christian," Jade snapped, snatching her arm away from him.   "What are you talking about?"

"Jade," Marcus said in that deep, cool delivery of his.   Jade looked at him.   He shook his head, his attractive face revealing nothing.   But it revealed enough, because Jade backed off. Christian looked at Gina, to see if somebody else saw the influence Marcus was beginning to have on Jade. Apparently she did because Gina, he noticed, was staring at Marcus.

Dutch walked down the hall to the second of the two small guest rooms. As soon as he entered the open door, he saw Sam. She was standing at the window, her back to the door, in a pair of sheer pajamas. Dutch walked to her.

"Hello, Sam," he said to avoid scaring her.

But when she turned her small body toward him, and he saw the confusion, the pain, the anxiety on her face, his heart plunged. *Poor Sam*, he wanted to say, but knew she would hate him if he did.

"What are you doing here?" she asked, surprised to see the president standing there.

She looked more like Jade's sister than her mother, it seemed to him, as she stood there in her skimpy bed wear. "Our daughter gave me a call," he said.

"I don't know why Jade does that," Sam said. "I told her I was fine. I just have rough nights sometimes. I woke up talking to myself from some dream and she blows it all out of proportion. She knows I have nights like this sometimes."

Dutch was now standing beside her at the window. He leaned against the frame. "You weren't seeing people?" he asked.

Sam turned slightly sideways, her braless breasts jiggling. Dutch looked back into her face. She smiled. "I was joking with her. I told her I saw dead people, yes, I told her that. But I also told her that she was going to be one of those dead people I saw if she didn't get out of this room and leave me alone."

Dutch would have smiled. But he was concerned about Jade. "And she knew you were joking?"

"Of course she knew! She knows how disagreeable I can be when she makes a fuss. I hate that with a passion."

That sounded exactly like Sam. "Understood," he said.

Then she turned again slightly, and one of her sizeable breasts almost spilled out over her top. "And here you come running. You have really spoiled her, you know that?"

Dutch looked slightly alarmed. "Spoiled her? Me? I wouldn't think so."

"You don't have to think so. It's a fact. Jade has you wrapped right around her little finger."

Dutch didn't know what to say to that.

"Anyway," Sam said, "how are you? You look tired."

"I'm okay."

"That wife of yours treating you right?"

Dutch remembered just how right Gina had treated him not that long ago. "Yes," he said.

"Good," Sam said. Then she smiled. "You're a good guy, you know that?"

Dutch stared at her. He'd had his issues with Sam in the past, especially the way she seemed so enamored with Jade's ex-boyfriend, that asshole Henry Osgood. But he always had this romantic view of Sam as odd, yes, disagreeably so. But a good woman in the end. "You're a good girl," he said.

Sam smiled. "My compliment sounded like a statement," she said. "Yours sounded like a question."

Dutch laughed, and then placed his arm around her waist, pulling her to him. He liked her.

Gina walked down the hall and stood at the door just as he pulled her against him. They seemed to be laughing at some joke. They seemed to be old friends from way back sharing an innocent joke.

Close old friends.

Jade walked gingerly up the hall behind Gina. When she peered past her into the room and saw her father with his arm around her mother's waist, and she saw that Gina saw the affection her parents were demonstrating, she smiled grandly. This was what she was talking about, she wanted to shout.

When Gina turned her way, realizing she was behind her, that smile of Jade's, that grand, conniving smile, was gone.

Later that same morning, Dutch woke up far later than his usual early rise. He knew it was Gina. She had undoubtedly refused to allow any wake-up calls given his exhaustion. Which he appreciated. But it was a new day and world events weren't about to stop churning because he was tired. He sat on the side of the bed, completely naked and still heavily sleepy, picked up the phone, and checked in with Allison.

Overnight there had been a crisis in Iran, she said, with violent protests erupting there that may require some covert resistance support by the U.S.. The Secretary of Defense was requesting an emergency meeting of the principals, and Dutch agreed. "Within the hour," he said, and hung up the phone.

He dragged himself out of bed, brushed his teeth, showered his body, and shaved his face. With his groomer's assistance he was soon dressed immaculately in a double-breasted suit, and his hair was freshly cut and styled, not a strand out of place.

He stood in the mirror and stared at himself. Even though he was hardly some young stud, he was still being voted, year in and year out, as the sexiest politician in Washington, with Crader McKenzie always close behind. But Dutch was beginning to feel his age, and the burdens of all those years of edge-living behind him. Now he wanted the quiet life, with his wife and his children.   No more lights, cameras, or action for him.

But Gina was right, he thought with a smile. Don't turn on the light, she once told him, and then complain when it gets too bright.

And just thinking about Gina, and the way they made love not all that many hours ago, began to give him yet another hard on. And just like that he wanted to taste her again. Which was amazing. But he craved her whenever she wasn't in his sight. Sometimes, late at night, he'd wake up with his fingers deep inside of her. And more than once Gina jokingly said that her clit was going to frizzle up into nothingness if he didn't stop fondling it so much.

And although he was already nearing the time for his meeting to begin, he stepped out onto the terrace of the presidential suite anyway, hoping to get a glimpse of that woman of his.

And there she was. Out in the privacy-fenced off area of the White House lawn designated as Little Walt's play area. She and Little Walt were raucously playing catch football, with their staff of nannies, led by the head nanny, looking on. But just seeing his wife and his child warmed his heart. He even forgot about his meeting and took a seat on the terrace. He crossed his legs and eagerly watched them at play.

Gina would throw a child-sized football to Little Walt and Little Walt would attempt to catch it. He, of course, would miss it every single time, but then he would pick it up and attempt to throw it back to his mother. The boy was smart for his age, but he wasn't exactly athletic. His aim would miss the mark badly every time. But Gina, in her cute pink warm-up suit, her short hair in a gorgeous free-flow, would jump up and down and applaud his effort and make him feel like the most beloved child in the world.

And Dutch sat there staring at her. She was such a special person to him, a woman with a heart of gold. She was strong, and opinionated, and sometimes angered him in ways very few others ever could. A weak man couldn't be her man. She'd run all over a weakling. And although many people were certain that Dutch had Gina well in hand and that there was no way she could ever run over him, he knew better. He knew, unlike anyone else knew, that Gina was his weakness. His strength, which was legendary to every world leader on the face of this planet, was mush when it came to Gina.

And then it happened. Little Walt actually caught one of Gina's passes. Forget that she was practically standing toe to toe with him when he caught it, the fact that he caught it was definitely cause for celebration. And Gina was celebrating, jumping up and down again and giving Little Walt a high five that knocked him on his rump. Dutch laughed so loud that Gina somehow heard it and looked up. When she saw that Dutch was sitting there, she pointed to him.

"Look, Daddy's here," she said to Little Walt, who was asleep when Dutch arrived home early this morning. Little Walt saw his daddy waving at him on the terrace and he took off, with football in hand, running like a pint-sized sumo wrestler. Gina, laughing herself now, took off behind him. The nannies took off behind them.

Little Walt held the rail, but was able to waddle his way up the side stairs that led to the second-floor terrace. Gina was right behind him, in case he slipped, but allowed him to make the journey all by himself.

When he made it onto the terrace, he dropped that football and took off toward his father, his little arms outstretched. Gina took note how Dutch, thrilled to see him too, remained in his seat with his arms outstretched. Any other time and Dutch would have been out of that chair and would have run to hug his son. He didn't this time, Gina suspected, because he didn't have the energy to do it.

But he did lift Walt into his arms as soon as he made his way to his chair.

"Daddy!" Walt said as Dutch lifted him up. Dutch had his eyes closed as he felt the bones of his son, inhaled the sweet smell of his son.

"I missed you," he said as he looked at Walt, at his thick brown hair, at his stunningly adorable green eyes.

"Me and Mommy miss you too."

"Bet I miss you more."

"We miss you a lot. Mommy says you were in hell."

Gina laughed. "Hel-sin-ki, Walter. Not hell. Helsinki."

"Which amounted to the same thing," Dutch said, considering the zero results those three intense days of talks netted. He looked at Gina. Gina was leaned against the rail staring at him.

"You okay?" she asked him.

"I'm sure the papers this morning are ravaging the summit and my lack of influence there."

"They are," Gina admitted, "but who cares? Are you okay?"

Dutch smiled, the lines of age appearing on the side of his eyes. Only Gina bothered to ask. "I'm okay," he said.

Then, coming up the side stairs, was Allison, Dutch's former press secretary and new chief of staff. "Good morning, Mrs. Harber, Mr. President."

"Good morning, Ally," Gina said.

"Good morning," Walt said.

Allison smiled, bent slightly down. "And good morning to you, too, Mr. Harber. How are you this morning?"

"Fine," Walt said.

Then she looked again at the president. "Your cabinet has assembled in the Situation Room, sir," she said.

Gina saw a look of drain appear in Dutch's eyes. "Thank-you, Ally," he said and then patted

Walt on the hip. "Up, you," he said. "Daddy has work to do."

"Daddy working?" Walt asked as Gina lifted him off of Dutch and held him in her arms.

"Yes, babe," Gina said. "Daddy's working."

"Daddy always working," Walt said. And although it was cute and funny and Allison grinned, neither Dutch nor Gina cracked a smile. It was one of the worse aspects of their life in this DC fishbowl. It was hardly funny to them.

Dutch reached over, kissed Walt on the forehead, and kissed Gina on the lips. "You two stay out of trouble," he said, and then proceeded to leave the terrace. Allison proceeded to follow him, but Gina stopped her. "Could I see you for a moment, Ally?" she asked as Dutch kept going.

"Of course," Allison said. She knew she was chief of staff today because Gina had fought for her promotion. She, in truth, felt just as much loyalty to Gina as she did to Dutch.

Gina motioned to the head Nanny, who immediately began to come. "Go with Nanny, Walter," she said to her son. "Mommy has to go to work, too."

"Mommy working?" Walt said as the Nanny took him from Gina.

"That's right," Gina said.

"Mommy not always working," Walt said and Gina and Allison laughed.

"That's exactly right, too," Gina said.

When the nannies and Walt left the terrace, Gina invited Allison to a sit down. After they both sat down, Gina didn't waste any time.

"I want you to clear the president's schedule for the remainder of the day," she said.

This request threw Allison. The First Lady had never interfered this way before. "Clear his schedule?"

"Clear his schedule. I can't just sit by and let this happen. He's dead on his feet, Ally, couldn't you tell that?"

She could. "I understand, ma'am, but he has ten more meetings today alone. And I'm talking meetings with a lot of foreign dignitaries."

"I understand that. Every day when he's in town he has tons of meetings with all kinds of people, I get it. But I saw that look of drain in his eyes, Ally. He can't keep going like this, I don't care who he has to meet." Gina then stood up, which prompted Allison to stand, too. "Clear his schedule," she said again. "Y'all aren't killing my husband."

Allison had never seen Gina so determined. And she suddenly realized if Dutch was her man she'd feel the same way. Ten meetings in one day practically every day of the week was ridiculous anyway. "Yes, ma'am," she said. "Consider his schedule cleared."

Gina smiled. She knew she could count on Ally. And then she left the terrace, determined to plan just the right getaway for Dutch.

CHAPTER FIVE

Marcus Rance sat on the sofa at the Osgood mansion and looked at the tall, straight back of his host. He looked over further, at a tall man in a wheelchair, paralyzed from the neck down. He had not been introduced to Marcus, but it was obvious that he was Dr. Henry Osgood, Jade's ex-fiancé who supposedly attacked her, prompting Dutch to attack him. In fact, the guy's father, Marcus's host, was treating the one-time big shot surgeon as if he wasn't his son, but nothing more than another piece of the furniture.

This was awkward as hell for Marcus, and if Dutch and Gina would have acted right he wouldn't be here at all. But the way they treated him. The way they said he couldn't stay at the White House. Oh, no, he wasn't good enough to stay there. Not around their precious little boy. Dutch even put it more bluntly than that: they really didn't know him from Adam, Dutch had said. He wasn't having a stranger around his wife and child, he had added.

A stranger. That was the way he had put it. He called Marcus a stranger. It was true, they really didn't know the character of the man, just that he may have been wrongly imprisoned for a crime he didn't commit. But Gina was his half-sister. How the hell was he some stranger?

And Dutch kept going. He said he would be more than happy to bankroll him a little house in the city of his choosing, and to help him find employment. But even that sounded like an insult to Marcus. It sounded as if the big-shot Dutch Harber was telling him that he'd help him out, but only on a small scale. He'd help him find a little house and a little job. Like hell, Marcus thought at the time. His half-sister was the First Lady and his brother-in-law was the POTUS, and their talking *little*?

He squirmed around on the sofa just thinking about that shit. A little house? A little job? Were they fucking kidding? This was his chance to make it big, to capitalize on their monumental success, and he wasn't going out like some chump idling away the rest of his days in some little row house on some little job somewhere. He wanted big and bigger. To hell with little! If it wasn't for Jade coming to his rescue and asking him to come stay with her and Christian until he could decide what he wanted to do, he would have went off on that Dutch motherfucker right then and right there. He didn't like his ass anyway!

He and Jade would talk about it for hours on end, especially while Christian was gone to work. But Marcus had to play it cool with her too. She loved that daddy of hers. Loved him to death. But she hated Gina. So Marcus played up that distaste for Gina angle whenever he was talking with Jade. She wanted Gina out of her father's life, and her own mother in his life, from what Jade was telling him. So that was what he focused on. He didn't have any great love for Gina anyway, or anybody else if truth be told, but it was Dutch he couldn't stand. It was Dutch's ass he wanted to kick.

One night, before they left for Helsinki and while Christian was still at work, Jade told him that she had a plan.

"A plan to do what?"

"To get rid of Gina."

"A plan to get rid of her?" Marcus had said with a chuckle. "What would you know about a thing like that?" He was seated on the sofa in Jade's small living room. He had a bottle of beer in his hand, his shirt wide open, revealing his brown-skinned, lean physique. She was seated in a chair, had a glass of wine in her hand, and wore a very sheer short set.

"I know more than you think," Jade said mischievously.

"Okay," Marcus said, checking out that fine body of hers, that gorgeous brown skin, that pretty face. "So what's your plan to get rid of the president's wife?"

"You," Jade replied.

"Me?"

"Yes, Marcus, you. You can get rid of her for both of us. You have access. And you have skills. Let's be honest here. You used to be quite the criminal."

"I used to sell drugs, don't get it twisted. I never did any of this plotting and scheming you're talking about. So I ask you again: what's your plan?"

Jade reached into the pocket of her shorts, pulled out a piece of paper, and tossed it over to Marcus. It fell on the floor. Marcus just sat there.

"Aren't you going to pick it up?" he asked her.

Jade smiled. Time to play one of their games again, she thought. Games, she also thought, that she loved playing with Marcus.

She therefore stood up, went over by him, turned her ass to his face and picked up the paper. Before she could stand up, Marcus grabbed her and sat her on his lap. On the dead center of his lap. She felt his hard-on as soon as she plopped down.

"You like?" he asked her, and drained down more beer.

"I like," she said with a smile. "But about my plan?"

"Yeah," he said as he sat his bottle on the side table and lifted her slightly. He slung her shorts and panties completely off. He spread her legs and began rubbing her furiously.

Then he began unzipping his pants.

Jade almost sighed out loud when she felt his cock fling out of his pants and jut against her bottom. "Don't you want to know about my plan?" she asked him, her voice already changing.

"Yeah, yeah, in a minute," he said as he shoved his dick inside of her as if he'd been preparing her for hours, when he'd hardly prepared her at all.

She winced at the pain, she wasn't wet enough yet, but Marcus didn't care. It wasn't about her, anyway.

He began to stroke her slowly for only a few seconds. They never spent any appreciable time on gyrations. They got in and they got out. And Marcus had no intentions of changing the routine now.

That was why he started pounding her. He was going one speed and one speed only. There was no finesse in his game. He pounded her so hard, and the idea of it felt so good to Jade, that she became wet instantly.

It became so good to Marcus that he tossed her down onto the sofa, her ass up, and laid on top of that ass. He started pumping her so hard that his balls were ramming against her. He started pumping her so hard that his dick started releasing within minutes. He knew it wouldn't take long. Because with Jade it was all about the cum. He just wanted to come. He didn't give a damn about foreplay or making her feel loved or making her cum. He just wanted to come.

And he came. Deep inside of her. He straightened his body like an arrow to let it all come out. He began to push in harder, to get every drip out. And it kept dripping and dripping and dripping. Marcus learned early how to experience every drip out.

Jade came too. It didn't take but a few strokes with Marcus. Christian was good. He knew how to do her too. But Marcus knew how to do her better. The fact that he didn't wait for any build up, the fact that it hurt and then felt so good, the fact that his dick was much bigger than Christian's, although Christian had a big one too, was a complete turn-on to her.

When she came, and when Marcus strained out his final drip, he collapsed on top of her. And laid there, attempting to regulate his breathing again.

"Goodness girl," he said between breathes. "You know how to do old Uncle Marcus." They both knew that they weren't blood kin at all, but they played on it just the same.

And then, within seconds, he pulled out and was off of her.

She put back on her panties and shorts, and he zipped back up his pants. That was their routine. A quick in and a quick out, most every night that Christian was working late at the White House. Jade, Marcus was beginning to realize, was the easiest lay he'd ever had. He didn't even have to ask anymore.

"Now can we get back to business?" Jade asked as she handed him the paper. She was now seated beside him.

Marcus grabbed his beer off of the side table and looked at the paper. "Thurston Osgood," he said. "Who the hell is that?"

"Henry Osgood, a surgeon, was my ex- fiancé. Thurston is his father."

Marcus chuckled. "They sound like a couple of assholes already."

"They are. Daddy found out Henry had violated me and he nearly killed him."

Marcus looked at her. "Really?"

"Really. Daddy can be something else if you cross him."

Marcus glanced back at that paper. He saw that in Dutch Harbor too. He saw that edginess in him. It concerned him, but it didn't worry him. Hell, he was edgy too. He wasn't scared of no Dutch Harbor. Bring it on, motherfucker, he inwardly said.

"So what about this Thurston Osgood?"

"He's willing to pay."

Marcus looked at her. Money was the name of the game now, as far as he was concerned. "Pay for what?"

"For Gina's head on a platter, as he puts it."

Marcus frowned. "Girl, what are you talking about?"

"If you get rid of Gina, he will pay you, Marcus. He will pay you millions."

Marcus's heart began to pound. "Millions?"

Jade smiled. "I have your attention now I see. But yes, he will pay you three million dollars if you take Gina out. And I know y'all have the same father, and that, to say the least, could be awkward."

"Like hell. She don't mean shit to me." That wasn't entirely true, as Gina actually meant more to him than anybody else. But that wasn't Jade's business. "Not when you're talking about three mil."

Jade laughed.

Marcus decided to play it up. He wanted Dutch's head, not Gina's, on a platter, but he would go along with Jade's hatred for now. And then turn it around.

"When Dutch said I wasn't good enough to stay in the White House," he said, "Gina didn't come to my defense. She just sat there and let Dutch kick me out. Talking about I was still a stranger to them. And then they didn't even want me to come here."

"Gina was the one," Jade said, although Marcus knew it was more Dutch than Gina. "She was the one talking about getting you a place of your own. As if they still think you might have killed those people in that drive-by."

"But back to this three-million-dollar deal," Marcus said. "What does he want me to do?"

"He'll have to tell you that," Jade said. "I'm just relaying the message. He heard you aren't all that tight with your sister so he figures you can be bought."

Marcus smiled. The only person who could have told him that lie was Jade. But it played on her hatred all the same. "Hell, yeah, I can be bought," he said.

For the right price, he also thought, any man could.

And that was why he was now sitting in the Osgood mansion. Thurston Osgood was standing at the window with his back to Marcus. And his son remained a non-entity in the room.

Thurston turned around and looked at Marcus. He was a tall, wiry, gray-haired man with small, blue eyes and liver spots all over his face. He was elderly, in his seventies easily, but he was as agile as a panther.

He walked over to Marcus and sat down in the chair oddly placed directly in front of the sofa. They were within inches of each other.

"Let me be clear," he said. "I don't like you. I think you're the scum of the earth. After all your sister did to get you out of that prison, and for you to turn around and be willing to do this to her, says a lot about your character."

Marcus studied Thurston. He knew exactly what he was after. That killer instinct. He had to be sure. "What character?" Marcus asked. "I'll sell my newborn baby if the price is right. What the fuck I care about some half-sister I barely know?"

Thurston nodded his head. Good answer, he thought. But he still wasn't sure. "Did you murder those people in that drive-by shooting?"

"Hell nall."

"So it was true?   You were wrongfully convicted?"

"Yes. That's true."

"You didn't participate in that drive-by?"

Marcus smiled. "I didn't say I didn't participate. I said I didn't do the shooting."

Thurston smiled. What a slime ball. "And you never ratted on the person who did do the shooting?"

"And never will. I don't snitch. And never will."

"I need your access to get rid of somebody."

"I know. Jade told me. You want to get rid of the First Lady."

"No, Marcus. No." Thurston said. "It's the president I want. I had to say that it was Gina Harber I was after in order to get a certain party on board, if you know my meaning."

Marcus nodded. Jade wouldn't harm Dutch even if her life depended on it. But Gina? She wanted that bitch dead. It wasn't even close.

But Marcus was on the same page with Thurston Osgood. It was Dutch he was after, too.

"You have access, Mr. Rance," Thurston continued. "And you also have what it takes to get the job done. I'm an old man now, with all kinds of ailments. I won't be around much longer. There's little they could do to me. Death, in fact, would be more tolerable. But what that so-called president did to my son is not acceptable."

Although Marcus was reasonably certain that the man in the wheelchair was Thurston's son, he wanted to see what Thurston had to say. "Your boy, your son, he's not dead, is he?" Marcus asked.

"Oh, no. Death would have been too easy for him."

Thurston looked over at his son, but didn't acknowledge him. "Dutch Harber knows what he's doing," he continued. "He wouldn't kill him. He just made him a human vegetable. He can only sit in a wheelchair, with support of course. He can't feed himself, he can't talk, he can't clean his own shit. My brilliant surgeon son can do nothing on his own now. Thanks to Dutch Harber. And for that, Dutch Harber has to pay. Before I die, he has to pay."

He looked back at Marcus. "I would do it myself, but I have no access. You do."

Marcus stared at the man. How the fuck did he expect him to kill the President of the United States? He was under around-the-clock guard. "How do you figure I accomplish this feat?" he asked his potential sugar daddy.

"Find a way," Thurston said. "If you find a way and get it done, a private jet will be waiting for you to take you and your millions to wherever you want to go. Free to live however you want to live."

Marcus leaned back. With Jade's access, under the guise of Gina as target, he might just be able to pull this off. Yes, he thought. He just might be able to do this.

"But not for three mill," he said to Thurston. "If you want POTUS, it will have to be ten."

Thurston stared at Marcus. Said nothing for a long time. Then he nodded his head. "Good," he said. "I would have thought I had the wrong guy if you would have accepted three. And yes, Mr. Rance, I do want the president. You are so right about that. I want Dutch Harber to suffer. Yes."

He looked at his paralyzed, drooling son again. "I want it more than I've ever wanted anything in my entire life."

As soon as the doors to the Situation Room were opened and Dutch and his National Security Advisor, Ed Drake, emerged, Ralph Shaheen, the head of the Secret Service, commandeered him.

"Hello, Ralph," Dutch said jovially. He and Shaheen went back many years.

"How are you, sir? Advisor Drake?"

"What brings you over here?" Dutch asked him.

"Your wife requests that you come with me, sir."

"Ooh oh," Ed said jokingly. "I know who's staying after school."

Dutch smiled. "Tell her that I have another meeting. I'll get with her later today."

"Now, sir," Ralph said. He was a big, burly man, brown hair, brown eyes. Midnight black skin.

"Excuse me?" Dutch said. He wasn't accustomed to his orders being questioned.

"Your wife said I was not to take no for an answer, sir."

That didn't sound like Gina. But it was also rare for the head of the Secret Service to come and approach him this way, too. Dutch therefore excused himself from Ed, and he and Ralph headed down the corridor.

"What's going on, Ralph?" Dutch asked as they walked.

"Your wife will explain, sir."

That wasn't exactly the answer Dutch was going for, but he let it slide. And followed Ralph down the back stairs of the White House, along a long corridor he wasn't all that familiar with, to the private parking area. An older model Chevy Malibu was parked in the garage. Dutch looked at Ralph, who proceeded to get into the backseat. Dutch bent down, looked through the window, and saw that Gina was behind the wheel.

He opened the passenger side door. "What do you think you're doing?" he asked her.

"Get in," she said cheerfully.

Dutch was surprised by this display, but he got into the car anyway. He looked down, at the nice twill pants and matching blouse she wore, and then he looked into her face. "You don't intend to drive this thing?" he asked her.

"Of course I intend to drive it! Why do you think I'm behind the wheel? Before I married you I actually had to drive myself everywhere I went."

"No kidding?" Dutch said, kidding with her.

"For real though. I'm a great driver."

Dutch didn't doubt that she was. But just sitting there, with his wife behind the wheel of a car, caused him to realize just how much of a cocoon they lived in, and had lived in. He'd never seen his own wife drive a car. And, he realized, she'd never seen him drive. His presidency had forced them to be chauffeured around the entirety of their marriage.

"So where are we going?" he asked her.

"A nice, quiet place."

"And what about our son?"

"He's with LaLa and Crader. He's fine." She then took his hand. "I just want you to relax. And get some rest."

Dutch certainly couldn't argue with that. He needed rest. Plenty of it. But again, the world didn't stop just because he was tired. "Babe, I can't just take off like this," he said. "I am booked solid with meetings today."

"Not anymore," Gina said with a wry smile.

Dutch stared at her. "What do you mean not anymore?" Then he thought about Ralph in the backseat, and the fact that Gina was so certain of herself at this moment. "You cancelled my meetings?" he asked her.

This was the moment that she knew all along would make or break their little getaway. "I did tell Allison to cancel your meetings, yes I did. But just for today, Dutch. You deserve a break."

"So you went behind my back and had my chief of staff cancel every single one of my remaining meetings?" He asked this with shock in his voice.

Gina braced herself for his wrath. But she knew he needed to get away if only for a night. She was willing to take the hit. "Yes," she said. And then she waited for his reply. And waited.

"Well?" she said.

Dutch looked at his wife. "Thank-you, Jesus!" he said with a grin.

Gina exhaled with joy. "Ready to blow this joint?" she asked, cranking up.

Dutch laughed. "I was born ready," he said.

"I must say, sir," Ralph said, "this is highly irregular."

Dutch laughed. "I already figured that out, Ralph," he said.

"Oh, wait," Gina said. "Take off that coat and tie."

Dutch didn't question it. Gina had his best interest at heart and he wasn't fighting it. He removed his coat and tie. Gina handed them to Ralph Shaheen, and Ralph then handed her a blue and white letterman jacket with a baseball cap.

"Put these on," Gina said, giving them to Dutch.

Dutch smiled and he did as he was told. When he zipped up the jacket, Gina began laughing.

"What?" he asked, genuinely confused.

"You look like a gym teacher," she said.

"Just drive, you," he said.

And she did. Gina, Dutch, the head of the Secret Service, and a full contingent of agents left the White House as if they were ordinary staffers leaving work. Dutch continued to stare at Gina, still amazed to see her behind the wheel, and this wall of security escorted the president and his driving wife out of Washington, DC, across the Potomac, and into Virginia.

They drove down a secluded street, through an electronic privacy gate that was now manned by the Secret Service, and onto property that Dutch knew all too well. It was a lakefront home he purchased years ago, when he was a United States Senator. Gina drove around the horseshoe driveway and parked in front of the circular steps.

Dutch just sat there. Amazed. Gina looked at him.

"I haven't been here in years, Gina," he said.

"I know. I had the caretaker spruce up the place and the Secret Service did their security sweep. And here we are."

Dutch felt so blessed to have her in his corner. He almost choked up right then and there, but he wasn't about to put on that kind of emotional display in front of Ralph Shaheen. They got out of the car and went inside the home. Ralph got out too, and headed around the vast property to ensure airtight security.

As soon as Dutch and Gina entered the home, and Gina moved away from him, he pulled her back. And pulled her into his arms.

"One rule," he said as he kissed her on the mouth.

She enjoyed his taste. "And what rule is that?" she asked him.

He kissed her again, this time more passionately. "No clothes," he said between kisses. Gina grinned. She didn't like rules, but she was certain she could live with that one.

CHAPTER SIX

"Whoa, not so fast, you," Dutch said as he pulled Gina back and wrapped her in his arms. "I said no clothes."

Gina looked at him. "You didn't mean now, did you?"

Dutch began kissing her neck. "Why not now?"

"But Dutch," Gina said, lifting her chin to give him full access, "this is supposed to be a time for you to relax."

"What do you think I'm doing?" he said, as his kisses trailed down to her chest. "This is very relaxing."

"Dutch, come on. You know what I mean. I want you to do absolutely nothing for a change."

"You smell so good," he said as he began unbuttoning her blouse. "You always smell so good." He opened her blouse and then pulled her bra cups down below her hefty breasts.

Gina inwardly smiled. Once those breasts of hers were exposed, she knew there was no stopping him now.

"Now this is even more relaxing," Dutch said as his hands began to fondle her breasts in tight squeezes. And then his mouth joined his hands as it began to press soft kisses all over her juicy breasts.

"I don't think a day has gone by in our entire marriage, if you're not out of town, that you aren't fondling my breasts." Gina said this with a smile, as she continued to lean her head back in enjoyment of Dutch's fondling. "Are you aware of this habit?"

"Well aware," Dutch said, becoming too sensually aroused to smile, although inwardly he was delighted.

"I do believe my breasts have gotten bigger because of your fondling. Is this possible?"

Dutch had to smile at that. He glanced at his wife. "What do you think?" he asked. But when he looked into those insightful eyes of hers he felt a surge of love shoot through him. And he began kissing her on the mouth again.

Gina wrapped her arms around his neck and returned his passion. They stood there, in the middle of a home Dutch once used as his bachelor pad, and groaned and smacked in unison. Their heads turned one way, then another, as they couldn't get enough of the other's taste. She could feel his penis becoming more and more aroused as it pressed against her while they kissed.

But eventually Dutch, as Gina knew he would, moved his mouth back to Gina's breasts. And once again he was fondling them and kissing them. He took her fully distended nipples whole into his mouth, and then pulled them as far from her breasts as they would extend. Then he bunched both breasts up together and licked his tongue across their juicy mounds in a way that caused Gina to feel tingles of fire deep inside her vagina.

Dutch began unbuttoning and unzipping her pants as he licked her. Gina held onto the back of his head as he lifted her and carried her to the first seat they came upon, which was an arm chair. He sat her down in the chair, removed her pants and panties completely, with her heels still on. He then pulled her butt to the chair's edge and spread open her legs as wide as they could extend. And in this position, where her pussy was completely exposed and wrinkled and ready for his exploration, her legs were able to extend in the extreme.

"I know how you smell," Dutch said as he got on his knees in front of her and removed his letterman jacket. Then he lifted his shirt off of his ripped, tanned body in one adroit sling off, and tossed it across the room. "Now," he continued, his face moving between her legs, "I want to know how you taste."

Gina felt that tingle again as he began rubbing her pussy with his fingers. His eyes were looking at it, admiring how all of him was always able to fit so snugly into that tiny pink passageway of wonder. And then his mouth took over, as she was happily anticipating it would, and he began to taste her.

Gina leaned back in the chair and closed her eyes in delight as he licked and sucked and chewed into her. If some of those blue-haired old ladies who loved themselves some Dutch Harber knew what their president was doing at this very moment, they would blush red in astonishment. At least some of them would, Gina thought with a smile.

And Dutch was doing her exactly right. She felt his tongue rub against her inner fold over and over, as if he couldn't get enough of her taste. She felt his fingers open her wider and his entire mouth move in, sucking on her in the kind of suctions that made her lift in her seat. This black-haired man was giving her that thrill again, and she couldn't imagine how she ever lived without it. And he didn't ease up. Dutch didn't roll like that. He would always take her further and further until she was just at that point of release. And then, and only then, as if he could sense it himself, he would ease up.

But he wasn't ready to ease up yet, as he continued to mouth fuck her. "Your taste," he kept saying, "I love how you taste!" And he couldn't get enough of her taste, and her smell, and everything that made her his wife. He knew Gina now. He knew every inch of her body now. And that was why he continued to drive her to the point of cum, just on the tip of tipping over. And just when she gave that quiver, he stopped. And stood up.

Gina opened her eyes with a lustful gaze as he began unbuckling and then unzipping his pants. When he pulled his pants and boxers down, and his dick jutted out like a stiff, thick rod, her mouth began to water. His dick was as much a part of her now as her own womanhood was. That was how often he had it inside of her. That was how badly she craved it when it wasn't inside of her. And as he stepped out of his pants and boxers and kicked those expensive clothes aside as if they were rags, her need to have him inside of her again was electric.

She should have been ashamed of herself. Here she was, bringing him all this way to take care of him. But within moments of their arrival he was already taking care of her. And taking care of her as only he could, she thought, as he moved toward her, placed his hands beneath her ass, and lifted her legs, wide as they could go, into the air. He guided his dick to the entry of her womanhood, teased her with his gorgeous pink head, and then slid it in with that preciseness that always stunned her.

She wanted to cry in joy when she felt the friction of his entry. It was always tight and explosive, as if he was breaking through a thicket of moist cunt. And then, once he broke through, it broke her. Because his strokes became like darts against a board: on target every time he slid into her. Dutch was standing there, completely naked, his ripped stomach pushing in and out as he pushed in and out of her. He was working it as hard as it could be worked, his eyes hooded with the sensual gratification every time he saw his dick thrash into her pussy.

He leaned down and took her breast in his mouth as he fucked her. His penis was saturated with her moistness and it couldn't stop thrashing into her. He wrapped his arms around her, and she wrapped her legs around him as his mouth couldn't stop sucking her breasts with every pound. He never dreamed a day that began with an emergency national security meeting could end up being a day where all he had to do was pleasure his wife. He could do that with his eyes closed. Because he wanted to please her. He wanted to make her cum so badly that every thrash was his toast to her. This one's for you, baby, his every stroke made clear.

Until he stroked so hard, pushed in so far, that she couldn't bear up any longer. He had her on the brink ever since he stopped mouthing her. Now she was beyond the brink. She came. Her body began to spasm in that euphoria of feelings that she didn't think she could handle.

"Let it out, Gina," Dutch was ordering her. "Don't you dare hold back. I want you to let it all out!"

And she did. She let it all out. He held her tighter as she held nothing back. He could feel her heartbeat quicken as she throbbed against his rod. It was an electrifying throb that soon caused him to suddenly experience what felt like a body blow and arch in a pulsating thrust of his own, a throbbing that almost took his breath away. And he came too.

His cum poured out of her like thick milk, trailing down her thighs and saturating her inflamed folds. He'd put a fucking on her she wouldn't soon forget. That was always his goal. To give her better than he gave before. And from the way Gina's eyes smiled back at him, from the way she kissed him and looked at him, he knew he had accomplished his goal.

His penis remained inside of her, still pulsating in heavy strikes, waiting for the feelings to end. He looked at Gina and kissed her again. He kissed her with a long, sweet kiss. And when the pulsating finally stopped, he pulled out of her. He lifted her into his arms, and carried her to the bedroom. Where, he already knew, he would fuck her again.

Later that evening, Gina lit the candles, looked over her hard work once more, and then took a long exhale. She was so nervous she could hear the syncopated beats of her own heart. She walked slowly down the long corridor that led into the study. Dutch had been on the phone ever since they woke up from their long, wonderfully restful sleep. But he promised tonight would belong to them. Gina's prayer was that her meal, her hard work, would start the night off right.

She opened the door of the study slowly and peered inside. And there was Dutch, in his jersey and jeans, his silky black hair flopped down around his forehead like a sexy bang. He was still on the phone, reviewing a document that had been faxed over and writing notes all at the same time. Gina momentarily stood there, admiring the view.

But then she realized her food was getting cold.

"Excuse me, Mr. President," she finally said. It was clear to her that Dutch didn't even realize that she was in the room.

Dutch looked up. And his beautiful green eyes went from their usual intensity to a softer, warmer glare. He lifted two fingers and motioned for her to come on in.

"Yes, Ally, that's what I'm saying," he said into the phone. "All twelve. Right. And I want it on my desk when I get back. Right. Okay, dear. Good work. And you take care. All right." And he hung up. And then leaned back in his swivel chair, looking at Gina.

She, too, wore jeans and a jersey but she wore hers with that Gina flare he loved. She looked particularly attractive, he thought. The only thing out of place was that apron around her waist.

"Hello there," he said. "What can I do you for?"

"Dinner is served," she said.

Dutch looked at that apron, and then back into Gina's dark brown, anxious-looking face. "Dinner cooked by you or brought in by the White House Chef?"

"Cooked by me," Gina said with a smile. Then she frowned. "Oh, Dutch, don't look so terrified. Chef Grady has taught me a lot. I can cook now."

Dutch still looked doubtful. He loved Gina but she was the worse cook he'd ever encountered. Just awful. Just thinking about some of those dishes she cooked up in the past made him nauseous.

"Just come on," she said, walking around the desk and pulling him up by the hand. "You'll see."

Dutch allowed himself to be dragged away from his work, down the corridor, and into the spacious dining room. The candles were lit, the food was already on the table, and Gina was anxious. To his relief the food at least looked edible.

He pulled her chair out and then took a seat at the head of the table. "It certainly looks good," he said as he placed the napkin onto his lap. "What is it?"

"Risotto and lamb."

They bowed heads, said their prayers, and then Dutch took a bite. Gina stared at him as he did. He chewed, nodding his head.

"Wow," he said.

Gina began to smile. "Is it good?"

"That's the thing," Dutch said between bites. "It's even worse than the way you used to cook."

Gina's heart plunged.

Then Dutch smiled. *"Psych!"* he said with a grin.

"No, you didn't," Gina said, happy that he liked it, but angry that he fooled her. She took her glass of wine and flung it at him.

But Dutch, still laughing, moved his body just enough that he only endured a glancing blow. And when she stood up, to come after him again, he took off running. She grabbed his glass of wine and took off after him.

Dutch had never laughed harder in his life as Gina chased him through the dining hall, through the living room, and out onto the lanai. When he ran out of real estate, and was backed up to the massive pool, she kept coming.

"I've got you now," she said, laughing too. "You crafty little---"

But she threw the wine and missed, because Dutch jumped into the pool, splashing her. He laughed so hard as she stood there, her arms flailed out as she withstood the chill of suddenly being drenched. She looked at him. He was laughing hysterically and pointing as if he got her good.

But then, to his surprise, she jumped into the pool, too. "You forgot you taught me how to swim," she said to him, and gave chase.

Dutch took off swimming around the massive pool too. And lap after lap they swam, Gina chasing Dutch, laughing like kids.

Dutch dived underwater, to avoid her, and she didn't realize he had swam near her until she felt a firm slap against her bottom.

She laughed and took off. The hunter was now the hunted, as they swam around the pool until their arms hurt. And when they agreed on a truce and came together, Dutch, happy beyond measure, moved to kiss his lovely wife. And she moved to kiss her lovely husband. But she turned her head as soon as their lips were to meet. *"Psych!"* she said, laughing, and swam off again.

Dutch shook his head in amazement. He really had him a dynamo on his hands. But he should have seen that one coming.

He didn't dwell on it, however. He was having too much fun. He gave chase again.

That night, in the library, Dutch sat on the floor with his back against the chair, and Gina lay prone on that floor, her head on his lap. Dutch sipped wine, stroked his wife's hair, and read over some documents that couldn't wait. Gina understood that world events waited for no man, so she didn't complain too much. A little, but not too much. They were both in bathrobes now, after showering together and then finishing their dinner, and now all they wanted to do was enjoy the easiness of life away from DC.

Finally, he put the documents aside, along with his glass, and laid behind his wife and they spooned.

Gina snuggled her ass against his front. "I hope you're enjoying yourself."

"I'm beyond enjoying myself, babe. I'm having a blast actually."

Gina smiled. "Good. That's what I've wanted. You deserve a break today. After all that time in Finland, and then Jade calling you in the middle of the night for essentially nothing at all. You deserve to have a day off."

Dutch kissed her on the back of her neck. He pulled her closer against him, his hand on her waist. "What do you make of Jade?" he asked Gina.

Gina shrugged her shoulders. Talking about Jade these days wasn't something she was comfortable doing. Dutch was so protective of her, as if he was still blaming himself for not being there for her childhood, and she rarely wanted to go there. "She loves her daddy, what can I say?" she said.

"I'm concerned about her," Dutch said. "She's getting to behave a tad too inappropriately."

"How so?"

"She's constantly in my face, constantly comparing me to her husband. And while we were in Finland she was standing in my bathroom when I got out of the shower." Dutch couldn't bring himself to say it, but he remembered distinctly how she stared at his dick when he stepped out of that shower, and how she attempted to lean her body against his. He understood she was still starved for his affection, he understood that. But she was beginning, he also understood, to take it too far.

"And the way she would cry and fall into my arms," he continued, "and then she'd forget the tears so easily and smile as if she's the happiest girl in the world. I'm getting concerned."

"Jade has always been different, Dutch. Maybe not as odd as her mother, but different. There's a part of her that's the same girl that came to us from South Carolina. She was sweet, and kind, and a devoted schoolteacher. I always felt as if she was trying to overcome something even then."

"Her childhood undoubtedly," Dutch said as Gina's ass against him awakened his dick. "Her physically absent father and emotionally absent mother. She didn't stand a chance."

Dutch lifted the bottom of his wife's robe and slid his penis between her legs. He rested it at the front entry of her folds, prepping her.

"Yeah, but something changed in her. She used to like me. We had, I thought, a very good relationship. Now she treats me as if I'm her enemy. I don't know what happened to her."

"My job happened to her, as it's happened to all of us. She suddenly realized she was the daughter of the President of the United States and she started behaving as if she had this sense of entitlement."

"The press doesn't help," Gina agreed. "They love to talk about the president's beautiful, sexy, drop dead gorgeous daughter. And she loves it."

"You know what I love?" Dutch asked.

"What?"

"This," Dutch said and shoved his penis into her with one hard shove.

"Whoa!" Gina reacted to his shove. And just like that they were at it again.

"I'll say it again," Gina said as he fucked her.

"Say what again?" Dutch asked as he pulled her small frame closer against him to get the full angle he needed to thrash into her. She was soaking wet already.

"The way you go at that thang of mine," Gina said with a smile. "You're going to wear it out, Dutch!"

"That's the idea," Dutch said as his hips thrust harder and harder against her, leveraging his penis. "Every time I fuck you I want you to feel as if I'm wearing you out."

"Oh, you are," Gina said sensually as his gyrations increased, creating loud mashing sounds of saturation between his dick and her pussy. "I want you to know beyond a shadow of a doubt that you belong to me," Dutch said, pounding her. "And I'll kill the first prick who even thinks about touching you!"

And Gina didn't doubt it, she thought, the way he was going at it. She loved the way he went at it. She loved his style. She loved the fact that this man could fuck her all night, as he had all day, and she still would want more. There was no way, no way at all, she thought, that she could ever tire of

Dutch Harber's sex. He could wear her down, he often did that, but he could never wear her out.

And as they came, and eventually settled into another restful sleep, she knew her instincts had been right: get the man out of the fishbowl, and the fishbowl would get out of him.

CHAPTER SEVEN

That next morning, Dutch was refreshed and back at work. He was seated behind the historic Resolute Desk in the Oval Office, his suit coat over the back of his chair, reviewing a series of press conference cliff notes. He knew that everything from his trip to Helsinki, to the Israeli-Palestinian conflict, to the floods in Tennessee would be hot topics when he faced the press later that morning. His staff knew not to disturb him frivolously during this review. Because he wanted to be prepared. To Dutch Harber, the secret to a successful encounter with the always skeptical DC press corps, was always preparation.

That was why he was more than a little perturbed when his desk intercom buzzed. He leaned forward and quickly pressed the button.

"Yes?" he said to his secretary. *Why are you disturbing me*, he wanted to add, but didn't. She was only doing her job.

"Your son-in-law is here to see you, sir," she said.

Dutch hesitated. He was relatively certain what this visit was about. "Send him in," he said, and leaned back in his big, executive chair.

Christian entered the office cautiously. He was getting more comfortable with Dutch, but his heart still pounded every time he was in his presence.

And it wasn't just because Dutch was the most powerful man in the world. It was Dutch himself. He could have been a farmer on a farm as far as Christian was concerned, and he'd still be intimidated by the man.

He walked slowly toward the big desk. Unlike his father-in-law, who always dressed immaculately, the suit Christian wore fitted him as if it were a size too big. And although Christian had biceps almost as muscular as Dutch's, his oversized outfit concealed his remarkably fit physique. What it didn't conceal, however, was his lack of confidence. Because when Dutch looked up, he almost stopped in his tracks.

"Good morning, sir," Christian said nervously, his blue eyes in a hard stare at the president.

"Good morning," Dutch said and looked back down at his notes. "What can I do for you, Chris?"

Christian didn't expect to launch right into it, but he also knew the president was a very busy man. "I came by last night to talk with you, but you and the First Lady weren't available." Christian waited for an explanation regarding their whereabouts. None came. He swallowed hard. "It's Jade," he finally said.

Dutch hesitated, and then looked at him. Christian was a mild-mannered young man in his mid-twenties, and Dutch was a tough, older man who'd never been mild about anything. But he knew they had one thing in common: they wanted

DUTCH AND GINA 6

the best for Jade. That was why he always listened intensely to Christian's concerns.

Christian had hoped Dutch would ask for more information, or something to get him going, but he just sat there. Which he usually did whenever Christian was ranting about that wife of his.

"I'm concerned about Jade," he went on. "She's becoming so disrespectful, sir. Especially in front of Uncle Marcus and her mother. And other people too. She won't listen to anything I have to say, no matter what it is, and I just don't know what to do about it. Like early yesterday morning. I told her not to call you. I told her you needed your rest. Even Miss Redding told her not to call you, that she was just fine. She just had a bad nightmare, she said. It was nothing. But Jade phoned you anyway."

Dutch continued to look at him. It was damn uncomfortable for Christian. Dutch's big green eyes always seemed so laser-focused. But he kept on. "Even when you and the First Lady came over, and you went into the back to speak with her mother, she tried to go back there with you. I told her no, she should let you handle it. But she snatched away from me. Then Uncle Marcus tells her not to go back there and she doesn't go. It's like he has more sway over her than I do, sir."

Dutch leaned back in his chair. Christian didn't realize it, but Dutch was seriously considering every word he spoke. "You're coming to me with this why?" he asked.

113

That wasn't exactly the ringing bell of support Christian had hoped for. But he didn't buckle. "I'm coming to you because you have more sway over her than any human being on the face of this earth. I'm coming to you because I have nowhere else to go."

Dutch could feel Christian's distress. And he couldn't argue with his logic, either. Jade was certainly enamored with her father, even Dutch would have to admit that.

He tossed his review sheets onto his desk. "How do you think she feels about you, Chris?" he bluntly asked his wide-eyed son-in-law.

Christian had to think about this. "You mean Miss Redding?"

"How does your wife feel about you?" Dutch corrected.

"Oh, yes sir. I see. Well, I think she . . . I'm not sure but I think she loves me. Somewhat."

Dutch frowned. "She loves you somewhat? What the hell kind of answer is that?"

"What I mean is that Jade isn't a touchy-feely kind of woman. She doesn't like to discuss love and stuff like that. She never even wants to have. . ." Christian was turning beet red. He didn't mean to reveal so much. He looked at Dutch.

Dutch stared at him. "She doesn't have sex with you on a regular basis?" he asked.

Christian was embarrassed, but the truth was the truth. He exhaled. "No, sir, she doesn't."

"How often?"

Christian thought about this. "Used to be once a week or so. But now that Uncle Marcus is staying with us, it's been kind of like never."

Never? Dutch could hardly believe it. How could the young man take it? All Dutch's life he had to have it, and certainly more than once a week at that. Even now if his dick wasn't sliding inside of Gina's warm folds at least every other day he was antsy. And this kid was standing before him talking about getting it maybe once a week, or now not even that regular? Dutch could hardly believe it. That daughter of his needed a swift kick in the ass for torturing young Christian the way she was doing.

"I don't know, sir," Christian continued, attempting to make sense out of what Dutch saw as nonsense, "but she just doesn't seem to find me very interesting anymore."

Dutch thought about that response. Was careful in his reply. "Does she find Marcus Rance interesting?" he asked.

"Oh, yes, sir," Christian replied without hesitation. "They get along great. They play cards together and cook meals together and talk about all sorts of things. She loves his company."

"Does she?"

"She does very much, sir. I mean, I like Uncle Marcus too. He's a real upfront guy. He talks about the old days when he was a drug dealer and it's real fascinating how he's turned his life around. I mean, Uncle Marcus used to be a straight-up gangster." Christian said this with a laugh, as if he, too, was mesmerized by the attractive Marcus Rance.

"And Jade asks him all kinds of questions," Christian continued. "I talk about my job here at the White House and she's bored to tears. Marcus talks about his days selling drugs and she's blown away with excitement. I don't know, sir. I think she's just thrilled to have her uncle in her life."

"The thing is," Dutch said, leaning forward, his voice measured and slow, "Marcus Rance is my wife's half-brother, that's true. They do have the same father. He is most definitely some kin to Gina. But he is also, most definitely, no kin to Jade."

Dutch said this and stared intensely at Christian, to gauge whether or not the young man understood. And on some level Dutch could see that he did get it. He did understand the significance of having a smart, savvy, attractive former drug dealer like Marcus Rance all up in his wife's face. But on that deeper, *I'd better do something about this* level, Dutch could see that the poor kid was completely out to sea.

Which meant, Dutch knew, that he would eventually have to intervene.

His desk intercom buzzed again. Dutch pressed the button again. "Yes?" he said with more than a little impatience in his voice.

"I hate to disturb you again, sir, but the Vice President would like a word."

Dutch exhaled. Forget any prep work before his press conference, he thought. "Send him through," he said.

"I'd better get back to the First Lady's office, sir," Christian said. He was an aide in the First Lady's office. "I hate to keep bothering you about my personal life."

"No bother, Chris. Not at all. But I do expect you to pay attention, son, and to keep control of your home."

"Keep control of it, sir?"

"Yes, Christian." Dutch actually thought of a proverb from the Holy Bible: *he that troubleth his own house, shall inherit the wind*. "Keep control of your home," he warned him again.

Christian understood. And was about to say so, but the vice president entered the room. Christian spoke to Crader, and then left.

"Crader, my man," Dutch said as he gave up any chance of reviewing notes this morning. Crader McKenzie rarely did casual visits. If he came, he usually had a darn good reason.

He, in fact, walked around the desk to Dutch's side and sat on the desk's edge, next to the president, facing him. Like Dutch, he wore expensive Italian suits. But unlike Dutch, his suit already looked rumpled.

He handed Dutch the newspaper clipping Allison Shearer had received in the mail.

"What's this?" Dutch asked.

"Read it."

Dutch looked at the picture of Jim and Elvelyn Rosenthal. He read the entire article. Then he looked at Crader. "What's this?" he asked again. "Beyond a tragic plane crash?"

"The woman," Crader said. "She look familiar to you?"

Dutch looked at the woman again. "Can't say that she does. Who is she?"

"Remember Vegas 2000?"

Dutch had to think about it. "The millennium."

"Right."

Dutch thought harder. "We were in Vegas for some congressional meeting or whatever it was called. And you were the committee chairman."

"Right. But what do you remember about that weekend, Dutch?"

Dutch leaned back. "I'm sure we boozed and partied. That's usually what we did at those so-called getaways."

"Remember the woman that boozed and partied with us, Dutch? With you and me together?"

Dutch stared at Crader.

"As in the three of us together. You, me, and her." Crader said this and placed his finger on Elvelyn's picture.

Dutch looked at the woman again. Still didn't ring a bell. But that weekend did. He'd done a lot of shameful things in his bachelor days, and that boozy weekend was near the top of his list.

"So we banged her twelve years ago," Dutch said, tossing the article aside. "And now, unfortunately, twelve years later, she's perished. I hate to be callous here, but she wasn't the only one we banged, not even that weekend was she the only one."

"No, Dutch, that's where you've got it wrong. She was the only one. We screwed around a lot that weekend, you've got that part right. But with her every time. Sometimes together, sometimes individually. But it was always only her. Elvelyn."

Dutch looked at the photo again. Poor girl. She was just a plaything to them back then. A sex toy. He thought how he would feel today if some man treated his own daughter the way they treated this woman. Or the idea of some man treating Gina that way. Geez. He'd want to kill the guy. He looked again at Crader.

"Somebody sent you this?"

"Sent it to Allison with a note for her to show it to me."

"To you?"

"Right."

"Did Allison see anybody or---"

"Nope. It was delivered to her residence as regular mail."

"To her home?" This surprised Dutch. "Then that would suggest somebody with familiarity with her."

"Right," Crader agreed.

"Which suggests the person had to have some very intimate knowledge of that weekend, and they also had to know Ally pretty well."

Crader stared at Dutch.

"Max?" Dutch asked.

"It has to be," Crader said. "He was the only other person there. He was the guy who coordinated her visit to our hotel room."

"Because we trusted him to be discreet," Dutch was remembering, "and to find a woman with a lot to lose, too, if our little get together was ever exposed. Yeah, you're right. She was some rich college student---"

"---whose father was a prominent banker or something in Vegas," Crader continued. "But she liked to get down and dirty, as long as the guys were hot. And I'm not bragging," Crader went on, "but they didn't get any hotter back then than Harber and McKenzie."

"You're bragging," Dutch said, "but I get your point."

"But it has to be Max," Crader went on. "Only four people knew exactly what went on in that hotel room: me, you, Max, and Elvelyn. Elv's dead. You and I are you and I. It has to be Max."

"But the timing is curious too, Cray. She just died a week ago. And now this clipping comes in the mail. Maybe she told a family member or friend and after her death they decided to send it to us."

"Maybe," Crader said. "It's a remote possibility. But my money's on Max Brennan. He's a snake in the grass. This clipping has that bitter, broken down old Max written all over it."

"Did you have the envelope and this clipping tested?" Dutch asked.

"Of course. I had it privately handled. But nothing's there. No unknown fingerprints or smears, nothing. The sender was meticulous. He knew what he was doing."

"Damn," Dutch said. This was all he needed. "So what is it this time? Some extortion scheme, what?"

"He wants something all right," Crader agreed. "But damn if I know what. I'm just concerned, that's all. Did that fucker record that shit?"

"Oh, come on, Cray."

"I wouldn't put it past him! We thought Max was loyal back then, somebody we could trust. We didn't know how low down and dirty he really was until here recently, Dutch. Think about it."

Dutch did think about it. "I understand what you're saying. And I wouldn't put it past Max to have recorded us, either. But what would it really prove? That we banged some female?"

"In our capacity as United States Senators at a retreat paid for by taxpayer dollars. And if he recorded both of us with her, at the same time, Dutch . . ." Crader stared at Dutch to make sure he fully understood the implications of such a video.

Dutch looked at his friend. He was only now getting the message. "You're going to run for president when my term ends, aren't you, Cray?"

Crader hesitated. Had to admit the truth. "I've been approached by more than a few wealthy donors and yes, I'm considering it."

"This video, if it exists," Dutch went on, "would end any chance you have of ever being elected."

"Hell, Dutch, this video could end any chance of my remaining vice president, or of you completing your own term! The American people may take a look at what we did with that young lady twelve years ago and conclude we're too morally corrupt to lead this nation."

"We were morally corrupt back then," Dutch said with bite. "That's for damn sure." Then he exhaled. "Okay," he said. "Keep trying to locate Max. Get an FBI assist if necessary. But quietly."

Max stood erect. He was glad to know that Dutch was taking this with the seriousness it deserved. "I'm on it," he said.

"And if they do locate him, we'll take it from there," Dutch continued. "We'll see if Max was as twisted then as he is now. But I don't think it's as dire as you're making it out to be, Cray. Just chill. Enjoy your wife. Enjoy your new baby. Find Max." He said this with that icy look in his eyes Crader was well familiar with. "And then we'll handle it."

Crader wanted desperately to tell the other side of the story, but he couldn't bring himself to go there. Besides, that newspaper clipping could be all about that weekend in Vegas twelve years ago, as he was hoping it would be, and nothing more. It seemed the only logical conclusion, since Max would know about that weekend too.

Nobody, not even Dutch, was supposed to know the rest of the story.

CHAPTER EIGHT

Gina sipped from her scalding hot coffee as she sat sideways, legs folded, at her conference table. Christian, LaLa, and three of her additional top staffers were also seated with her, their respective coffees in front of them. This marked LaLa's first day back to visit Gina's office, since she gave birth to Nicole.

"How does it feel to be completely back to normal again?" Gina asked her.

"Like new money," LaLa said with a smile.

"I'm glad you decided to bring baby Nicole to the Nursery over here rather than keeping her all by herself at Blair House."

"I want to be able to peep in on her all hours of the day. I wouldn't be able to do that at Blair, and do my job. I prefer to have my office here anyway, away from home."

Gina understood that. Little Walt was no newborn any longer, but she was still peeping in on him all times of the day too.

"Considering all you've gone through," Christian said, "you look great, La."

LaLa looked at him. She was still hurt that Jade had had a miscarriage. Christian, she felt, would have made an excellent father. But then again when it came to Christian, LaLa was always his biggest supporter. "You make it sound as if having a baby is a tortuous thing," she said to him.

"Well, isn't it?" he said to her with that innocent look on his face.

She smiled. "Hell to the yeah it is!" she said, and everybody laughed.

Madge, one of Gina's top aides, interrupted the gaiety. "Are we still on for the DC Rotary Club, Mrs. Harber? I need to give them an answer by this afternoon."

"Only if I can get in and out," Gina said. "Those gatherings tend to go on and on. And I still want to put in some volunteer hours at Bridge Gap. See if my brother cares to join me."

"Yes, ma'am," Madge said, writing furiously.

"How's that working out?" LaLa asked. "With Marcus going with you I mean?"

"Beautifully," Gina said. "In fact, they've asked him to become their community outreach leader."

This astounded LaLa. "Really? Wow, G, that's great. Marcus does have a way with the ladies." They both laughed. Christian turned slightly in his seat. Then LaLa asked: "How does Marcus feel about it?"

"He loves the idea," Gina said. "He told them yes immediately. Of course their board would have to agree, given his less than stellar background, but the executive director has every confidence. But Marcus loves the idea."

"Especially since the president had nothing to do with it," Christian said and LaLa looked at him.

"What do you mean?"

"He just doesn't like people doing things for him, especially the president. He feels his hard work got him the job."

"Oh, that's nonsense!" LaLa said. "If he wasn't the half-brother of the First Lady of the United States and if his brother-in-law wasn't the president, Bridge Gap wouldn't have allowed him to be a janitor in their center. I mean, let's be real here. The fact that he has these powerful connections, and could raise awareness about their organization, had everything to do with them making him their outreach director. Surely he realizes that."

Christian looked at Gina. He wasn't sure if Marcus realized it at all. And, in truth, Gina wasn't sure either. After that incident where Dutch decided to bar him from residing inside the White House with the rest of the family, he seemed to have developed a powerful grudge against Dutch. Gina fought behind closed doors on his behalf, she fought fiercely, but when Dutch made it clear that no way was he staying there and they told Marcus, they presented a united front. And although Gina still disagreed mightily with Dutch's decision, that was and always would be between her and Dutch.

The door to the office of the First Lady flew open and Allison Shearer, the president's chief of staff, came hurrying in.

"Turn on the TV," she ordered.

"What is it?" Gina asked.

"The president is getting brutalized."

"At the press conference?" LaLa asked.

"Yes! I mean he has been blindsided!"

Gina's heart began to pound. "About the summit?"

"Yes. They're calling his entire presidency a failure just because he couldn't broker an agreement on Europe's debt crisis. It's painful to watch, Gina. It's painful to watch!"

Christian quickly grabbed the remote and turned on the flat screen against the back wall. They all watched. And there was Dutch Harber, standing by the podium in the East Room of the White House. The press corps was packed in like sardines. And they were letting Dutch have it. It was as if Dutch was single-handedly responsible for the economic woes in Europe simply because he couldn't get the Europeans to agree to terms. Dutch remained cool, but Gina could see that Allison was right: he was under siege.

And it went on like this for a good twenty minutes. Question after question was an indictment of his leadership abilities. But then finally the subject matter switched from the Helsinki Summit. But it switched to an even greater potential blindside. And Dutch's cool exterior began to show some signs of cracking.

"Mr. President, what about Stephanie Mitchell?" a report from the AP casually asked.

"What about her?" Dutch asked, although he'd never heard of the woman. But he knew that the first rule in politics for a sitting president was never to admit total ignorance.

"According to our sources, sir, she says that her recently deceased sister, Elvelyn Rosenthal, knew you."

Gina looked at Allison. "Who's Elvelyn Rosenthal?"

"I don't know her," Allison said coyly, although she certainly knew of her from that newspaper clipping someone had mailed to her home.

Dutch, however, smiled, attempted to downplay his growing concern. "I know lots of people, Ed," he said to laughter. "You'll have to do better than that."

"How many people do you know intimately, sir?" Ed of the AP asked the president. This provoked murmurs.

"Before I was married," Dutch admitted honestly, "I knew many women. And I knew many of them intimately," he added.

"What about their children?" the reporter asked.

This stumped Dutch. And many others in the room. "Excuse me?"

"Stephanie Mitchell also asserts that you should be asked about Elvelyn Rosenthal's child."

Gina stared at the screen when a child was mentioned. Dutch's heart began to pound. A child? What child? Did he impregnate this Elvelyn person when he had her twelve years ago? But he wore protection back then. Didn't he?

"I'm sure I don't know anything about her child," Dutch said, his voice not as steady any longer.

"I'll be blunt, sir," a Reuters reporter chimed in. "Are you the father of Elvelyn Rosenthal's son?"

Dutch's heart began to pound. "I am not," he made clear.

"What makes you so certain, sir? Have you taken a DNA test?"

"Of course I have not taken any DNA test."

"Then what makes you so certain, sir?"

"I'm certain that I would know if I had a son out there," he said.

"You didn't know you had a daughter out there for twenty-three years, sir," the reporter pointed out. "And Mrs. Rosenthal's child is only eight months old."

Dutch was confounded. Eight months old? What the fuck?

"Did you cheat on your wife with Elvelyn Rosenthal, sir?" yet another reporter chimed in.

"No," Dutch chimed back.

"Are you certain, sir?"

"It's something that I would know, yes. I'm certain."

"Will you take a DNA test, sir?"

"No, I will not," Dutch said to murmurings from the press. "I do not have an eight month of child. That is a fact."

"Then why would Stephanie Mitchell suggest that you do? Why did she suggest we ask you about her deceased sister's child?"

"You'll have to ask her those questions," Dutch said. "Now are there any additional questions on the Helsinki Summit?" Although that Summit was a disaster too, it was far more appealing a topic than this minefield that he felt had just ambushed him.

"So you're telling us, sir," the reporter from Reuters said, "that you've never cheated on the First Lady, not one time during your entire marriage?"

"Have a nice day, guys," Dutch said, refusing to continue this madness.

But the questions about Stephanie Mitchell's allegations and Elvelyn Rosenthal's child and Dutch's alleged adultery were still flying, fast and furious, as he hurried away from the podium, and out of the East Room.

He burst through the doors so angrily and swiftly that his staffers could not keep up. He believed in preparation, that was always his calling card at these pressers, but even he wasn't prepared for this. Who the hell was Stephanie Mitchell, he wondered, and what was all of this talk about some *got*damn eight month old child? Only one man, he had a sneaking suspicion, could answer that question.

He made his way down the West Wing corridors toward that man's office: the Office of the Vice President. Staffers who were caught in the halls, not expecting to see the president in all of his fury, squeezed their backs against the walls as he stormed past. Crader was hurrying out of his office, putting on his suit coat, having just seen the press conference on television himself, before Dutch and his entourage made it anywhere near his suite.

When Dutch saw him in the hall, he stopped his progression. "In my office now!" he bellowed, and then made a beeline for the Oval.

Crader's heart was ramming against his chest as he made it down the hall, hurrying behind the president.

When they made it into the Oval, all of the aides knew not to follow. This was private, Dutch's actions made clear, as he slammed the door shut.

And they, Dutch and Crader, were alone.

To calm himself back down, Dutch walked slowly behind his desk and then sat down. He leaned back, his body slightly slouched, his fingers dabbing his lips as he stared at his vice president. Crader paced the floor, looking troubled and distressed, and made his way behind the desk too. He leaned against the desk, standing beside Dutch's chair.

He exhaled. "After Vegas," he began, "I continued to see Elvelyn."

Dutch continued to stare at Crader. He was one of the strongest, most courageous men Dutch knew. But when it came to women. . .

"We would meet up a couple times a year," Crader continued. "We'd have dinner." He moved his butt slightly. "Have sex," he added. "Then we lost contact for years. Nearly six, seven years. Until last year."

Crader slid his butt around again, as if his discomfort was increasing. "I was in Florida, at a dinner party with some friends, and Elv was there." He paused. "We hooked up that night and . . . spent the night. Then I hear from her a couple months later saying she was pregnant."

Dutch stared at Crader.

"Since she had just gotten married," Crader went on, "she knew she had to pawn the kid off as her husband's. But she believed the kid was mine."

Crader ran his hand through his hair. "I didn't know if she was blowing smoke up my ass or not, Dutch, that's why I never mentioned it. We didn't take any DNA test. I mean, yes, she came to me claiming it was my kid, but nothing was confirmed."

Dutch, however, didn't see the point of his contention. "Why would she claim it was yours unless she absolutely was convinced the baby was yours? All she had to do was pretend it was her husband's and keep you out of it, if she wasn't certain it was yours."

"I know," Crader said. "That's the thing. But she didn't want anything from me. She said I had a right to know, that's why she told me. But she said she was going to tell her husband that the kid was his, and it would never be questioned. Why would it be? As far as everybody were concerned, the child was Elv's husband. I mean, who would know any differently?"

Dutch looked at Crader. "You would know the difference. You, the father."

"*If* I'm the father, Dutch."

"That's easy to determine."

"And I will determine it. I'm not trying to shirk my responsibilities. I'm just. . . That poor child. It's just all so hard to digest."

"Why didn't you tell me about this, Cray?" Dutch asked, genuinely disappointed.

"I thought this whole thing was about that Vegas weekend, that's why I didn't say anything."

"You were *hoping* it was about that Vegas weekend. Because compared to this shit you're telling me about right now, that Vegas weekend, even if it was recorded, was a piece of cake." Dutch frowned. "A child's involved."

Crader knew he told the truth. He could say no more.

Dutch pinched the bridge of his nose. "What was the timeline?" he asked. "And you'd better not tell me you were engaged to marry Loretta when you had unprotected sex with that woman. Please don't tell me that, Cray." Crader said nothing, which astounded Dutch. "So it's true?" Dutch asked. "You were engaged to Loretta when you impregnated Elvelyn?"

"It wasn't planned, Dutch."

"What the hell's difference does that make?!" Dutch roared. "Of course it wasn't planned! Is that supposed to make it a little less fucked up by claiming it wasn't planned?!"

Dutch stood up angrily and walked to the window. He could throttle Crader he was so angry.

"I'm not making excuses," Crader said. "I messed up. I know I messed up. You don't have to keep telling me that. You can't say anything to me that I haven't already said to myself."

Dutch turned toward him. "Did you think about Loretta for even a second while you were fucking that woman?"

Crader ran his fingers through his hair. He frowned. "Of course I did. What do you take me for?"

"A damn fool and a cheating dog," Dutch said bluntly. "That's what!"

This stunned Crader. He fought back tears.

Dutch, however, had no sympathy. He gave Loretta away to this jackass. He had that long, drawn-out conversation with him about doing the right thing and keeping it in his pants, when even before they walked down the aisle he'd already fucked up. And the thought of it just angered Dutch more.

"*Got*dammit, Crader," he said, disappointment in his voice. "What were you thinking? How could you do that to her again?"

"It just happened, Dutch, all right? It wasn't like I went out looking for cunt! Me and Elv were through. I hadn't seen that woman in years. When we met up again we were just remembering old times. She was married for crying out loud!"

"And you were engaged!" Dutch thundered. He was so angry with Crader he wasn't sure if he could contain it.

"Yes, I was engaged, yes, that's true. But. . ."

Dutch frowned. "But what?" How, he wondered, could there be a *but*?

"But she was there, all right?" Crader admitted. "I was engaged to LaLa, I was happy, I was trying to do the right thing. When I met up with Elv at that party it wasn't like you think. We talked, enjoyed each other's company. But then one thing led to another thing and dammit, Dutch, what was I supposed to do?"

"Keep that fucking dick in your fucking pants!" Dutch said. Then he calmed back down. They both calmed back down.

"Where's the baby now?" Dutch asked.

Mention of the baby brought a new sense of dread to Crader. "With Elv's sister from what I could find out."

"This Stephanie Mitchell?"

"Right."

"Why would she think her sister's child could be mine?"

Crader shook his head. "I didn't think she knew anything about it. Apparently Elv had confided in her. Not just about me, but about that

Vegas weekend with you, too. Maybe the sister confused the two."

Dutch shook his head. All he needed. He ran his hand across his face. "And Loretta knows nothing about this baby?"

"Of course she doesn't know!" Crader snapped. "I can't just tell her something like this. Besides, I don't even know if the kid is mine yet."

Dutch shook his head. "How could you do this to your wife, man?"

Crader almost said she wasn't his wife yet, but even he knew how lame that would sound. "I told you being totally committed to one person wasn't going to be easy for me," he said, sounding lamer still. "I told you that. I'm not like you, Dutch."

"You're not like me?" Dutch asked, a frown on his face. "Don't you dare try to pretend that being faithful to the woman you love is some unobtainable goal that only the perfect man can achieve. Because you know what? There are no perfect men. I'm tempted every damn day, Cray. You know I am. But I don't run around fucking all these skirts that wanna fuck me! I can't do that to Gina. At some point it has to be about your wife, and not just you. What about Loretta?!" Dutch screamed.

"What about her?" Gina asked as she entered the Oval office unannounced. Both Dutch and Crader looked at each other. And Gina looked at Dutch.

"What about LaLa?" she asked again.

Dutch held out his hand. Gina walked over to her husband and placed her hand in his. "What's wrong?" she asked him. "And who's Elvelyn Rosenthal?"

Dutch looked at Crader. So Gina did also.

"She's somebody with whom I had a relationship."

Gina furrowed her brow. "You? Then why was the press . . . Okay, I'm sufficiently confused. At that press conference her sister was apparently running around telling reporters that Dutch is the father of Elvelyn's child, which is ridiculous," Gina added. "But. . . are you saying it's *your* child, Cray? That you have an eight month old baby?"

Crader's eyes fluttered. "That's what I'm saying, yes. That child could be mine."

Gina's heart dropped. "Oh, Cray, what have you done? You and La were married---"

"Engaged," Crader corrected her. But if he thought that would lessen the impact of his indiscretion, he was sadly mistaken. Gina fumed.

"The point is, Crader, as if you don't already know, you had promised to be faithful to her. After what happened with you and Liz Sinclair, you had promised LaLa, Cray!"

"I know I promised her, Gina. I know I promised her."

"Then what are you talking about? How could you father an eight month old? What, you asked LaLa to marry you, she gladly said yes, and then you went off to be with this Elvelyn person?"

"It wasn't like that," Crader said almost too low to be heard, his fight almost completely gone.

Gina shook her head. "Poor LaLa," she said. "How could you do that to her, Crader?"

"I know, Gina. I know, all right!"

"Careful, Cray," Dutch warned about his friend's tone toward Gina.

"I don't mean to raise my voice," Crader assured her, "but don't you think I realize how bad this is? I get it, G. LaLa may leave me, I understand that."

Gina stared at him. Was he that far gone? "She *may* leave you?" Gina asked. "Are you out of your mind? You asked her to marry you and then proceeded to screw some woman and have a baby with her, and you're saying to me that she *may* leave you? She *may*? She'd better leave your ass! Ain't no *may* in it!"

"Okay, babe," Dutch said, pulling Gina's back against his front, and rubbing her arms to calm her back down.

Crader ran his hand across his already rumpled hair. "I know I've done a terrible thing," Crader insisted. "And I know I deserve everything I'm going to get. I can't feel any worse than I already do."

"Who gives a damn how you feel?" Gina responded. "What about LaLa? What about *her* feelings? Because you obviously didn't give a damn about how she felt or you wouldn't have done what you did to her. Again!"

Disgusted, Gina moved away from her husband and began to leave. But Dutch pulled her back. Gina looked at him. "What are you doing, Dutch? I need to go see LaLa."

"Where is she?" Crader asked.

Gina couldn't even say another word to that man.

Dutch, however, looked at her. "Where is she, Gina?" he asked.

Gina exhaled. She knew she had to speak up now. "She got the baby and headed back to Blair House. She thought this Elvelyn Rosenthal was some new drama they were cooking up about you and me. So she decided to give us some space."

"Where is she?" Crader asked anxiously.

"Oh, you're so concerned now?"

"Gina," Dutch said in a warning voice.

Gina exhaled again. "She got Nicole and went back to Blair House."

Crader immediately hurried for the exit, his heart like a torrent of pain that hadn't even seen the half of it yet. LaLa, he knew, was going to be devastated.

"Why did you pull me back?" Gina asked her husband. "I should be there for La. I'm her best friend. I'm the one who cares about her. I should be the one to tell her."

"No, you shouldn't," Dutch made clear. "Crader is her husband."

"Some husband."

"I know, but he's her husband. He has to tell her."

"Did you hear that fool? She *may* leave him, he said. I wanted to kick his cheating ass."

Dutch pulled her closer against him and wrapped his arms around her. "Get in line," he said, his disappointment in Crader like a pang in his heart. And the thought of what this could do to Loretta made him even more disgusted.

"How could he do that to her?" Gina asked again.

Dutch knew how, he just couldn't understand why. Why would Crader risk so much for some piece on the side like that? Why would he do such a thing to their sweet, kind, never would so much as harm a flea LaLa?

CHAPTER NINE

Later that evening, Dutch and Gina were back in the Residence. After having dinner and putting Little Walt to bed, they sat together on a lounger out on their private patio, a blanket covering them and keeping them warm. The wind was blowing mildly across the White House grounds, creating a cool breeze that made them feel eerily peaceful. Although Dutch knew Gina was concerned.

"I haven't heard from LaLa," she eventually gave voice to her concern.

Dutch sipped from the glass of wine in his hand. His other hand was undercover, inside Gina's panties, gently rubbing the outer edges of her folds. Other than their excursion to Virginia, he rarely got to spend a quiet evening with his wife. There were always more meetings to attend. But tonight, he knew, he couldn't allow her to be alone.

"She'll call when she's ready," he said. "You have to give her some time."

Gina shook her head. "The idea that Crader would do something like that to her again, after losing her over this same shit the last time, just blows my mind. And now a baby is involved, Dutch. A baby." She shook her head again. "What is wrong with some of these men?"

Dutch kissed her on the forehead, leaned her closer against his hard frame. They both were lightly dressed in shorts and t-shirts, but both felt burdened. "Yes, some men think with the wrong head."

"But you were out there, just like Crader. You haven't been sleeping around and bringing home babies to me."

Dutch smiled. "I did bring a baby home to you. She was a grown baby, but still."

Gina had to smile at that one, too. Speaking of grown. "Miss Jade," Gina said. "That girl just loves her daddy."

Dutch hesitated. "Yes," he said and sipped more wine. Then he hesitated again. "I may get her an appointment with Dr. Katz."

"Dr. Katz?" Gina asked. "That same therapist you made me sit down with?"

"That's right."

"You think she needs therapy? Why would you think she needs therapy? Because of that mother of hers and the way she raised her?"

"And the fact that this father of hers wasn't a part of her life when he should have been."

"Oh, come on, Dutch. You didn't even know she existed until she was twenty-three years old. It wasn't your fault. I don't even blame Sam. She was young and she was scared. I can't even blame her."

"Understood. I don't blame her, either. But that doesn't mean damage wasn't done."

Gina understood that. "Jade isn't going to want to talk to any therapist, I can tell you that right now. Not Miss Jade."

"You didn't want to talk to one either."

"Yeah, but you made me talk to her. I don't know if anybody can make that daughter of yours do anything."

Dutch snorted at that. But then he dismissed the thought of that daughter of his and concentrated on this wife of his, instead. And specifically her folds that were getting wetter with every poke of his finger. He slid it inside and began to massage her more aggressively.

Gina leaned back and relaxed into his massage. It was nights like this, when she had Dutch's undivided attention, that she loved the most. Although it was tempered. Because LaLa wasn't far from her thoughts, too.

"What about Marcus?" Dutch asked. "You heard from him?"

Gina closed her eyes, the effect of Dutch's unique massage beginning to take control of her concentration.

"Yes. I invited him to my birthday bash next week."

"He accepted?" Dutch asked.

"Gladly. Why wouldn't he?"

"He wasn't exactly thrilled when I told him he couldn't stay here at the White House."

"Oh, Dutch, he understood that. We don't really know him yet. You're out of town often. You couldn't just leave him with me and Little Walt like that. It'll be like leaving a stranger in your home. And yes, we have Secret Service protection, but they aren't in our bedrooms like that. I think he understands it'll take some time for us to get to know him, and for him to get to know us, too."

"So you don't think he resents me?"

"Oh, he resents you big time," Gina said to laughter from Dutch. "He resents me, too."

This pronouncement, however, concerned Dutch. He stopped massaging her. "He resents you?" he asked.

"Yes, me, and don't stop."

"Why would he resent you?" Dutch wanted to know, as he began massaging her clit. "After all you've done for him?"

"When I was with Block by Block Raiders, I worked with guys like Marcus all the time. They get all of this help, and you and I would expect them to be grateful, and initially they are. But then they start believing that they're your family, and if you even think about treating them like the strangers that they really are, then they get seriously offended. They feel disrespected and they really do resent and hate you, I'm serious. I mean, it's as if you become their lightening rod. When you said Marcus couldn't stay at the White House with your wife and son, because you didn't know him like that, which was the truth by the way, that did something to Marcus. I don't think we realize just how slighted he felt."

"Well," Dutch said, sitting his glass of wine on the side tray, knowing he was getting too aroused to not get some from Gina. "If you ever see anything that concerns you about this resentment of his, you let me know."

"And why should I let you know?" Gina said with a smile as Dutch began to unbuckle and unzip his pants. "So you can go over and beat Marcus up for me?"

Dutch moved her on top of him, her back against his front, and began pulling down her shorts and panties as he did. "If he disrespects you," he said, "I'll do more than that to him."

Gina knew he meant it too. Henry Osgood was a prime example of that. And she couldn't even begin to imagine what he did to Robert Rand, another enemy of theirs. But then she forgot about Henry Osgood and Robert Rand and Marcus and Jade and focused on Dutch. And what Dutch's expert fingers were doing to her.

When he lifted slightly to pull down his boxers, and his cock flung out like a soldier at attention, big, thick, and rock-hard aroused, she wrapped her hand around it and began to stroke. His cock was now between her legs, jutting out fully aroused as if it was an attachment to her own vagina, and she stroked it hard.

"That's the way, baby," Dutch said as he leaned his head back and enjoyed Gina's massage. And when she leaned down beneath the blanket that covered them, and put her mouth on his rod, he began to shutter.

"Yes," he said breathlessly as he felt the full force of her expertise. "Yes. Gina, yes. Give it to me. Give it to me."

And Gina gave it to him. She knew how to give it to Dutch. And he continued, with his expert fingers, to give it to her.

Until he was too aroused, too full, to cooperate.

He lifted her onto his engorged penis, and slowly slid her down his long rod. He could feel her wetness began to coalesce around his cock as he entered her womanhood like a deep dive. And he kept sliding that baby in. He moaned it felt so good. It felt like sliding into home base, and he slid all the way home. This was exactly what he needed after yet another crazy-ass day, and he was going to enjoy this ride.

He placed his arms beneath Gina's thighs, lifting her up and down on his rod, so that she could enjoy the ride, too. And she rode him hard, the feeling of his fullness inside of her giving her that quivering sensation. And those slushing sounds of her wetness as his dick slid in and out, those sounds they knew so well, made both of them moan.

For a long time they relaxed and rode and moaned. She could feel every inch of his thickness, like a sensual thickness stuck deep inside of her, and the sweetness of that fullness gave her a fierce elation. They kept feeling as if they were on the edge of completion, but it kept on teasing them, over and over, until the tease became a thrill in and of itself.

The friction alone had them aching in pleasure. The unyielding slushing sounds of their lovemaking had them both grunting and groaning for more, louder sounds. And more kept pouring out of them.

They made love for the longest time. Until one simple movement, where Dutch's dick shoved into the deepest point of penetration inside of Gina's pussy, giving it an angle that made every muscle in his body quiver, and broke it loose for both of them.

"Oh, Gi," Dutch said in an almost grunting voice as he leaned against Gina's back and trembled with the impact of his release. Gina leaned back, against Dutch's chest, to absorb the impact of her own release.

And they came. In a fierce one-two surge of pleasure that left them both arching up and then pulsating down. It was so intense that it caused Dutch to grab his wife around her waist and hold her tightly against him, his heart pounding in near-hyperventilation. He knew what he had. Crader might not have realized what he had. But Dutch knew exactly the worth of this woman he had on his hands.

Later, after they had showered together, they decided to go up to the third floor Game Room and play some cards. There were large card tables throughout the room, some seating as many as eight to a table, but they opted, instead, for the more intimate two-person, fold-out table against the back wall. Gina had on one of Dutch's big shirts that dropped down to her knees, and Dutch had on a pair of jeans and a sweat shirt. He was drinking a can of beer, Gina was sipping pineapple juice, and both had already won a game apiece. This third game, Gin Rummy, belonged to Gina.

But the intercom on their card table buzzed just as she was about to proclaim her victory. To avoid having to endure that ridiculous crip-walking victory dance of hers, Dutch gladly pressed the button.

"Yes, Rogers?"

"Excuse me, Mr. President," the male voice on the other end said, "but Mrs. McKenzie requests permission to come up to the Residence. Is permission granted, sir?"

"Yes, of course it is," Dutch said.

Before he could even give that permission, however, Gina was already up and heading for the stairs that led to the second floor Residence, in total disregard of the fact that the only thing covering her was Dutch's big dress shirt.

He hurried after her.

Gina was already on the second floor and waiting in front of the elevators by the time he made it to her side. The doors clanged open and LaLa, with baby Nicole in her arms, stepped off. Her eyes were puffy, Dutch immediately noticed. From non-stop crying, he would venture to guess.

He removed baby Nicole from her arms as she all but fell into Gina's arms. Dutch held and bounced the pretty brown-skinned girl against his chest as Gina escorted the baby's mother to the West Sitting Hall.

Dutch carried the baby to the Nursery to be with Little Walt. It was no surprise to him that LaLa would come to them. He would have been disappointed if she hadn't. But he still couldn't help but wonder about his friend, and how that man had to be feeling right about now.

But he made the choice to screw that girl, Dutch thought angrily as the nannies on duty took control of Nicole. Now he had to live with the consequences of that screw up. But that still didn't stop him from worrying about his friend. And Loretta looked so distraught, he thought as he lingered in the Nursery watching his young son sleep. All because Crader had to have him a piece of ass. He used to be as reckless sexually as Crader. But eventually you have to get some balls and grow the hell up. They have children now, and wives. They can't keep do that old shit as if they were still in those relationships of convenience.

But what was done was done, Dutch thought as he made his way back into the sitting room.

There was nothing even Crader could do to change it now.

An usher was handing LaLa a glass of wine as Dutch arrived in the sitting room. Both she and Gina were seated, side by side, on the sofa.

"Will there be anything else, ma'am?" the usher asked Gina.

"That'll be all, thank-you."

The usher bowed slightly, said goodnight also to the president, and left. Gina looked almost as distraught as LaLa, Dutch noticed as he walked over to the sofa and also sat beside LaLa, placing her squarely in the middle. He put his arm around her waist, and she leaned against him. The tears she'd been fighting unsuccessfully ever since Crader laid it on her, began to reappear once again.

"We'll get through this, sweetheart," Dutch reassured her as he held her. Gina, who already had tears staining her eyes, rubbed LaLa's arm.

After a few moments of silence, LaLa sat erect again and wiped her nose with the tissue Gina had already provided to her.

"I hate bothering you guys like this," she said.

"There's no bother at all, young lady," Dutch said. "You're as much a part of us as our own children."

"Sometimes I feel like a child."

"Oh, LaLa," Gina said.

"I do. Since I had Nicole I've been feeling so emotional about everything. And now this," she shook her head. She didn't want to deal with anything like this right now.

"I just hate. . . I just .. ."

"You're welcome here anything, Loretta," Dutch made clear. "We love your company. We love you."

LaLa looked at the president and smiled. "Thank-you so much, Dutch. You've always been so kind to me. But I still hate bothering people over something so . . ." She frowned at just the thought of what Crader had said to her. Of what he had done to her. And more tears escaped.

"Oh, La," Gina said, tears falling from her eyes too. "You're like a sister to me. You could never be a bother to us."

"It's just that it hurts so much," LaLa finally decided to open up. "I thought we were beyond this. I knew Crader was still looking, and yes, I was worried about that, too. I was worried that those pretty girls with those perfect bodies would be too much for him to pass up. You know how Crader is, Dutch. He's always seemed to be attracted to the most beautiful, super model kind of women. Like Liz Sinclair. He seems to need those kind of women in his life."

"Don't make excuses for him, La," Gina warned. "I'm sorry but don't do it."

"I'm just being real, Gina. Those are the kind of women he liked."

"And? Dutch liked them too. But he didn't go out fucking every one he could get his hands on!

Talking about he needs them in his life. Crader ought to have his ass kicked, that's what Crader needs. Because if he was my husband and he pulled that shit on me, he wouldn't have to worry about sticking it into any other female. There wouldn't be anything for him to stick. Bet that."

LaLa looked at Gina in horror. Dutch's hand automatically touched his penis. They both knew that Gina's bark was worse than her bite, but when she did bite, watch out.

"I'm overstating it," Gina admitted, "but he just makes me so angry. He didn't have to do that to you."

"That's why it hurts so bad," LaLa said. "We were engaged, planning our wedding, and he was tipping out. He claims she was the only one, but I don't even know if I can believe anything he says anymore. Because for him to have gone out, after asking me to marry him, and have unprotected sex with another woman, impregnate that woman, and then expect me to get over it?" She shook her head. "That's asking too much of me. I don't know if I can accept that."

Gina was alarmed that she would have even considered accepting it. "Of course you can't accept it, La! What self-respecting woman could? And I know, sometimes it's not a matter of self-respect. It's the heart of the matter, I get that. But even if his ass was so in heat and he just had to screw that woman, he could have at least covered up. Come on now. That woman could have had

AIDS or something like that, and he could have passed it on to you, and to his own child! I'm sorry, La, and I know what Crader means to you, Dutch, but I refuse to let y'all minimize this. Crader fucked up and he fucked up royally this time. This ain't no Liz Sinclair, oral sex in the bathroom deal here. This could have been a matter of life and death."

LaLa knew Gina spoke the truth. She was tested throughout the course of her pregnancy and the baby was tested after birth, but Gina was telling the truth. She understood every word she was saying. And not long ago, if it was somebody else's man, she would have agreed with what Gina was saying. But it was no longer just some random man they were complaining about. This was her husband. The father of her child. It wasn't easy like that anymore.

Gina knew her friend was hurt. Beyond hurt. Devastated, even. But the worse thing she could do, Gina felt, was to pretend this wasn't as bad as it was. Because this was bad. Crader didn't just want that woman, he wanted her raw. He wanted her raw when he knew he was having unprotected sex with LaLa and was about to marry LaLa. That was disturbing on every level. He didn't think enough of her to cover up? This was messed up. Gina wasn't going to allow her best friend, a woman she loved like family, to minimize this.

She pulled LaLa into her arms. And LaLa cried in those arms.

Dutch leaned back, crossed his legs, and allowed the two friends to comfort each other. He knew that his wife didn't fully appreciate how tough it was for a man to remain faithful, and how it was a daily struggle. But every word she spoke to her friend was nothing but the truth. Crader's behavior was not only morally bankrupt, but he could have endangered the lives of his family. And that, in Dutch's view, was inexcusable.

LaLa eventually sat erect again, and wiped her nose again. She was getting a headache from crying so much.

"But you know what's even worse about this whole thing?" she asked after blowing her nose, her eyes still puffy and red.

"What could possibly be even worse?" Gina asked her.

"It's this feeling of inadequacy that I can't shake. It's this feeling of inevitability. Like, why wouldn't he cheat on me? Every man I've ever known has cheated on me. Each and every one of them. Why wouldn't Crader do it, too? That's how I honestly feel right now. I've never been that one special lady in any man's eyes, not really. I mean, I look at you, Dutch, and the way you look at Gina, and I've never had that."

Dutch's heart broke for LaLa. "What Crader did was deplorable, Loretta," he said to her. "But I know he loves you."

LaLa began shaking her head. "No," she said pointblank, refusing to ever again play those games. "Not the way you love Gina he doesn't. Because you can't love somebody the way they deserve to be loved and sleep with somebody else. I just refuse to believe that can happen. The idea that I would be in love with my husband but go and let some other man put his thang up in me? No way. I could never do that. Not ever!"

Tears began to reappear. "But Crader did it to me twice, Dutch. He cheated on me at least twice that I know of. Just like Dempsey cheated more than once and Jason and Michael and Patrick and every man I've ever been with. Every relationship I've ever had ended because the man cheated. Every one. That has to be some kind of record."

She attempted to smile, they all did, but not one of them could pull it off.

"But it makes me wonder too," LaLa continued, her face puzzled, confused. "It makes me wonder how many more times do I have to be dumped on before I realize these men see me as trash?"

"Don't say that," Gina said painfully.

"But it's the truth, G! It's the truth! For once in my life I'm facing the truth! I'm not pretty enough. I'm not smart enough. I'm not sophisticated enough. There's something that's not enough about me!"

Dutch quickly leaned forward, his elbows on his knees, his heart about to pound out of his chest. "Loretta, look at me," he said to her.

"Please don't tell me I'm over-exaggerating because I'm not. Please don't tell me that I'm this exotic beauty that any man would want because that's not true either. There's something about me that's lacking and these men see it in me and exploit it in me and then dump me!"

"Look at me," Dutch said again, his voice calm, measured.

LaLa, who respected Dutch above all others, looked at him. It was obvious that she was ready to dismiss anything even he had to say, but she looked at him.

"There is an inadequacy," he admitted, which caused Gina to look at him, too. "But it's Crader's inadequacy," he added. "Not yours. You didn't do anything but be an excellent fiancé, and then an excellent wife and mother to that man. You have nothing to hang your head down about. And you're right: men can be superficial pricks. I hear you. But don't you dare think it's because of you. Look at all of those beauty queen movie stars. Their men cheated on them too. Had babies by other women, too. The whole nine. I'm talking beauty queens like Halle Berry here. And these men didn't always cheat on them with other beauty queens, either. Some of those women they cheated with looked like pure hags! I mean they looked horrid. Because it's not about the woman, Loretta. It's never about the woman. It's about the man, and his own self-esteem."

LaLa, however, still wasn't convinced. "But you know Crader. He's full of confidence. He doesn't have self-esteem issues."

"Yes, he does," Dutch made clear. "Every man does. I do."

LaLa stared at Dutch. Was he saying this just to make her feel better? Or was he speaking the truth? "You?"

"Yes, me. I used to spread it around too. Crader has nothing on me."

"But then you met Gina and stopped thinking about doing anything like that."

"That's not true, either," Dutch admitted.

Gina looked at her husband.

"So what you're saying," LaLa asked, "is that you've cheated on Gina since y'all been together?"

"What I'm saying," Dutch said, "is that the fault doesn't lie with you. There are no easy answers here. It's complicated. It's almost mind-boggling how complicated this man/woman thing can be. It's not even about sex half the time. It's all about feeling of value to more than one person so that you can value yourself. Men are supposed to be the stronger sex, but when it comes to love and emotions and dealing with both, we couldn't be any weaker."

"You're Crader's best friend. You love him."

"I love him dearly," Dutch said. "That's why I'm so upset with him."

LaLa continued to stare at Dutch. "Should I divorce him, Dutch?" she asked with a plea in her voice. "Will he ever change?"

Dutch shook his head, a distressed look piercing his stark green eyes. "I can't answer that for you, my darling. You know I can't answer that. But I'll say this: Crader is a grown-ass man. He's my age for crying out loud. The idea that he still has to change, at his age, should answer that question for you, Loretta. Because you said it best. You have got to face the truth."

Dutch's words hit LaLa like a sledgehammer. And they just sat there, the three of them, realizing, by different degrees, the implications of those words.

Until knocks were heard on the door, and the usher stepped inside.

"Excuse me, Mr. President, but the vice president is downstairs and asks permission to come up to the Residence to see his wife."

LaLa looked crestfallen. She was already shaking her head. "No," she said to Dutch. "I can't."

Dutch nodded. Looked at his usher. "I'll handle it, thank-you," he said, and the usher left.

Crader stood impatiently in the empty waiting room. Although he had carte blanche throughout the White House, nobody was allowed to go up to the Residence without First Family permission.

And apparently, he realized after he was left waiting, Dutch wasn't giving his permission.

He knew it for a fact when Dutch entered the lobby looking oddly casual in his jeans and sweat shirt. Crader hurried to his best friend. He looked horrible, Dutch thought.

"Are they okay?"

"No, they're not okay, Crader. Of course they're not okay! But they're with me."

"I've got to see her, Dutch."

"No."

"I'm going to go mad if I can't see her!"

"Not tonight, Crader. You aren't seeing her tonight."

Crader took umbrage. "You can't stop me from seeing my wife!" he shouted. "She's my wife!"

Dutch just stood there, looking at him. Crader then moved away, raking his fingers through his hair, moving like a wounded animal caged in a wide open space. Then he looked at Dutch.

"What am I going to do?" he asked his friend, pain in his voice. "I can't lose LaLa!"

Dutch wanted to tell him he should have thought about that before he went to bed with Elvelyn, but he didn't go there. Crader already knew the stakes. "Go home, Cray," he said instead. "This is going to take time."

"You should have seen her face when I told her." Crader himself was staring into space, lost in his own disbelief. "At first it was as if she thought I was pulling her leg. It was as if she couldn't accept it, she just couldn't. As if she was . . . stunned witless. Then, when it dawned on her that I was actually telling her what an asshole she had married, she went into a kind of lost horizon. Like she couldn't figure out how I could ever do something like that to her. It was as if . . ." Crader looked at Dutch, his eyes troubled and distressed. "She believed in me, Dutch. And I blew it."

Dutch's heart dropped for his friend.

"What am I going to do?" Crader asked again. "I can't lose LaLa."

Dutch realized they would get no-where with this. It was a terrible situation and there was no other way around that fact. "Go home, Cray. Go back to Blair House. Work from there. There's nothing you can do here tonight."

"But will you at least talk to her? Will you tell her I didn't mean . . . That I . . ." Crader didn't know what to say.

Dutch exhaled. "Go home, Cray. You've got to give Loretta time to think, there's no two ways about this. You've got to give her time to decide what she wants to do."

"What if she doesn't come back to me?" He looked at Dutch with pure fright in his big blue eyes.

Dutch hated that Crader had put himself in this position, but that was the problem: he put *himself* in this position. "That's certainly a possibility," Dutch replied. "When you made the decision to sleep with Elvelyn you put that possibility on the table." Dutch frowned, staring at his friend. "You had to know that."

And of course Crader now knew it. Sadly, he knew. And although he didn't want to do it, he shook Dutch's hand, and left.

By the time Dutch made it back upstairs, LaLa was in the Nursery with her baby and Gina was standing at the lunette window in the back of the sitting room. When she turned and looked at Dutch, she faltered. He could see it as soon as she looked his way.

He opened his arms.

She ran into those arms and began to sob.

She cried for her closest, dearest friend.

CHAPTER TEN

The next day was a busy one as Dutch had three national security meetings in a row. By early afternoon he was seated in the Oval Office, a pile of files on his desk for his final approval, hoping for a break from the action. But Allison Shearer, his chief of staff, was standing in front of his desk requesting a presidential statement.

Dutch wasn't interested. "No statement," he said.

"But, sir," Allison pleaded, "the press is having a field day with this. The Vice President's office hasn't said anything constructive, except that they will not discuss the vice president's private life with the press. That's all their saying. What kind of statement is that?"

"A brilliant one in my view," Dutch said.

"But it puts the pressure back on you, sir. If the vice president doesn't come out and say I'm the one who had sex with that woman; I'm the one who may be the father of her child, then you're still the prime suspect. Shouldn't you at least release a statement saying that the child is not yours and you haven't cheated on the First Lady with this Elvelyn Rosenthal, or anybody else?"

"I'm not releasing any statements on that matter, Ally."

"Then they'll believe you may very well have been involved with Elvelyn Rosenthal."

"I don't care what they believe," Dutch said bluntly, glancing at Allison to make sure she understood: he was done with that conversation. Allison understood it.

"Yes, sir," she said. "Is there anything else you need me to do?"

"Matter of fact, do me a favor and hand deliver those files, those right there, to the DCI."

Allison didn't like it, mainly because she knew the press better than anyone. If you left this kind of scandal unanswered it always came back to bite you. But it wasn't as if she could argue with the president. She grabbed the stack of files. "I'll get these to him right away, sir," she said, and left his office.

When the door closed, and Dutch was once again alone in the Oval, he stood up and walked over to the elongated window. He stretched his back and looked across the White House grounds. The Secretary of State was sponsoring a press availability with the British Foreign Secretary in the Rose Garden, and everybody, including the Foreign Secretary, looked bored.

But Dutch had Crader on his mind. Why would he put Loretta through this kind of agony, was what he couldn't work out. It broke his heart last night when she sat in the Residence blaming herself, as if Crader's shit was all her doing.

When nothing could be further from the truth.

Dutch used to be unfaithful to girlfriends in the past, too, but he always made it clear up front that they were not in a monogamous relationship. And, more importantly, he didn't give a damn about those women and they didn't give a damn about him. They were just as Elvelyn in his past: a nice, warm body to fuck. Period. But the idea of him having that kind of attitude about Gina was unfathomable to him. He'd rather slit his own throat than have his wife and son fleeing his home because of pain he caused them the way Crader caused Loretta.

And then he started thinking about Gina. Although what he did with Elvelyn was twelve years ago, he had yet to tell her the full story of that shameful Vegas weekend. Mainly because he was embarrassed about it now. Gina was his number one fan. He wondered if what he did with Crader would be too much even for her. But he knew he still had to tell her. Max was still the wild card out there. He could still stir up trouble with some video or pictures of that Vegas weekend. No way could he allow his wife to find out about his sordid past through some breaking news report, or some headline in a tabloid magazine.

He left his office, headed down the West Wing of the White House, made his way into the East Wing, and then into the office of the First Lady.

"Is she in, Gwen?" he asked Gina's assistant as he headed for the office entrance.

"Yes, sir, she's in," the assistant replied.

Dutch leaned against the doorjamb and then opened the door. Gina, LaLa and Christian were seated around the conference table. She and Christian were working on the First Lady's speech at that upcoming awards ceremony at the Kennedy Center, and LaLa, from what he could make out, was keeping them company.

"Hello all," he said to them.

Gina looked up, a pair of prescription eyes glasses on her face. "Hi."

Dutch's heart squeezed with love when she looked up at him. "Got a few minutes for the old man?"

Gina smiled. Began standing up. "I think I can manage that."

Dutch glanced down, at her nice lavender pantsuit and how snugly it fit her, and then he looked at LaLa. She was smiling, but he could see the drain all over her.

"How are you, my darling?"

Her arms were folded. Her body was in what Dutch considered a closed position. Afraid, undoubtedly, to open up to anyone ever again. "I'm making it work," she said.

"That's the spirit. Keep that attitude and you'll be fine."

"Yes, sir," LaLa said as Gina arrived at Dutch's side. They were within an inch of each other. Dutch leaned over and kissed her on the lips.

"What's up?" she asked him.

"Walk with me?"

Gina smiled and then they left the office.

Christian closed the office door behind them, and headed back to the conference table.

"He must have something juicy to tell her," he said as he sat back down.

"Why would you say that?" LaLa asked.

"I've been working for the First Lady long enough to know that the only time the president bothers her in the middle of the day like this is for one of two reasons. Either he wants to take her upstairs to bed, or he wants to talk to her about something he believes is too crucial to wait."

LaLa smiled.

"I'm serious, La. Those are the only two reasons. Since he asked her to walk with him this time, I figure he must have something to tell her. But usually when he comes to get her, he takes her to bed."

"Well, I'll be," LaLa said, shaking her head. "You learn something new about people every day."

Christian laughed. "The president is so blessed," he said. "If I had a woman like the First Lady, I'd be one happy man."

LaLa looked at Christian. There was a time when he wanted to date her but she turned him down cold, mainly because of their ten-year age difference. She was no cougar, she announced. She, instead, got blinded by the light of Crader McKenzie. A man who even young Christian had warned was a bad risk as a boyfriend, not to mention as a husband. Now he'd cheated on her twice already that she knew of, and this idea that he may be the father of that baby was just too much.

But she couldn't think about that now. She'd fall to pieces again if she thought about that now. "You've got to cut Jade some slack, Chris," she said to her friend. "She's young."

"I know. But I'm young too." Young and in need of sex like he never dreamed he'd be in need of it. "I just don't understand her," he went on. "I just don't know where she's coming from. Like the way you and I talk and laugh and play around, I can't do that with Jade. I irritate her when I touch her."

"Irritate her?"

"Yes! We haven't had . . ." Christian began to redden.

But LaLa didn't get it. "You haven't what?"

Christian swallowed hard. LaLa really was his closest friend. Other than the president, she was the only other person he felt he could talk to. "We haven't had sex in I don't know how long, and it's beginning to bother me." Christian said this and looked at LaLa.

LaLa was floored. "You haven't had sex? Why not? Is there something wrong?"

"No, nothing, La, I declare there's nothing like that." LaLa would have laughed at his defensiveness, but he looked too distressed. And given her own situation, she knew what that felt like.

"Have you spoken with Jade about this, Chris?"

"Like every night, yeah," he said. "But it does no good. She throws the miscarriage in my face, as if it happened just yesterday. She even starts crying about it. I know it's tough for her, losing the baby, but it's tough for me, too. But I just feel like it's kind of fake the way she only brings up that baby when I bring up our sex life." He sighed. "I don't know. I told the president about it."

LaLa could only imagine the burdens Dutch bore. Every one of them were always running to him or Gina with their problems, when he probably had more than enough of his own. "What did he say?" she asked him.

"You know how he is. He listens mainly. But he did say he expects me to control my household. And he had a bunch of questions about Marcus."

"How's that working out for you? Having Gina's brother and your mother-in-law there? I'll bet that adds to the tension."

"Not really. They're both okay in my book. Sam is a little different, but I like her. Besides, her stay is only temporary. The president is helping her with some financial problems so she'll be going back to South Carolina soon. She'll be reopening her book store, I think. And Marcus is cool. We get along real well. Other than the president, he's the only one Jade will listen to."

"Well, I'm glad she listens to somebody," LaLa said in a voice that sounded doubtful.

Christian looked at her. "What about you, La?" he asked. "How are you doing? I never would have dreamed Senator McKenzie, I mean Vice President McKenzie---"

"Call him Crader," LaLa insisted. "You've earned the right."

Christian smiled. Forget the First Lady. If he had a woman like Lala? Now that would be paradise to him. "What I'm saying is that I never thought he would cheat on you. He seems to love you so much."

"I don't know about all of that, but yeah, it was kind of shocking to me, too. Especially now that a baby may be involved." She shook her head. "I don't know, Chris, I just wish. . ."

"What?"

LaLa smiled, looked at her friend. "I just wish Crader was more like you."

She'd never know how wonderful that made Christian feel. "Then he wouldn't be Crader, now would he?" he said, to shield his delight, and they both smiled.

But he knew exactly what she meant. Because he wished Jade was more like LaLa, too. He, in fact, secretly wished he'd never met Jade, and had been blessed to marry LaLa instead.

After a quiet, hand in hand walk across the grounds, Dutch and Gina ended up in the

Jacqueline Kennedy Garden. They walked along the perfectly manicured shrubbery until they were seated under the archway of the pergola, across from each other, at a small patio table. They were both formally dressed, he in his business suit and she in her pantsuit, creating a startling contrast to the relaxed greenery of the garden.

And Dutch told her all about that weekend in Vegas.

"I know it happened years before we were ever even dating, our first encounter notwithstanding, but I wanted you to know. Just in case there were photos out there, or videotape."

Gina stared at her husband. He was usually a straight shooter, but this time she felt as if she was missing something. "Why would it get in the papers?" she asked him. "You and Crader had sex with this Elvelyn person, but it happened twelve years ago when neither one of you were married or even engaged to anybody. Crader hooked back up with her, yeah, but you didn't. Right?" Gina asked this to be sure. Crader had stunned her with the way he so callously hurt LaLa. It had kind of rocked her faith for a hot second.

"Right," Dutch assured her. "It was just that weekend for me."

"Then why would it be news?"

"Because Max was there too. And he may have taken pictures, or videotaped it even."

"But I'm still not following you. All it'll show is you with some female during your womanizing days. The entire country knows that Dutch Harber used to be a player. Wham Bam Harber, remember? I still don't see how any of this would be news. Videotape or no videotape."

This was the part Dutch had dreaded. "But the tape may also show," he said slowly, carefully, "me, Crader, and Elvelyn. Together." He said this and looked at Gina. Gina was sharp. She'd get it.

And she did. Immediately. " A ménage e trois?" she asked him.

Dutch could already see the disappointment in her eyes. "Yes," he said.

"You and Crader screwed that girl together?"

Dutch exhaled. "Yes," he said again.

Gina was disappointed. No doubt about it. She always thought of Dutch as the good guy, as sort of the honorable rake when he was a player. Which, she knew, was nonsense. There was nothing honorable about slinging it all over town. But that was always how she viewed him. She even viewed him that way when they had their one-night stand in Miami Beach, years before they hooked back up permanently.

"Disappointed?" Dutch decided to ask her.

"Yes, actually," she replied honestly.

"Why?" he asked her, although he already had a pretty good idea. But he needed to hear it from her.

Gina folded her hand over her other hand, with both resting on the table. Dutch glanced down at her small hands, at that big diamond ring he had given to her, and then he looked back into her big, sincere eyes. "I thought you would have had more respect for women than to do something like that," she said.

Bam, there it was, Dutch thought. That was the reason he hesitated in sharing this part of his past with Gina. It would knock him off of that pedestal she had, rightly or wrongly, placed him on.

"I understand your disappointment," he admitted, "but it was consensual. She wanted it too or she wouldn't have been there."

"But maybe that was why her sister was accusing you of being the father of Elvelyn's baby. Maybe Elvelyn had told her sister about that weekend in Vegas, and then told her about her affair with Crader. Maybe the sister got them mixed up, or maybe she conveniently mixed them up."

"Why would she do that?"

"Because you'll get attention if the baby's father is the vice president of the United States. Yes, you're get some attention. But you'll get far more attention if the father of that child is the president."

"Ah," Dutch said, understanding Gina's thought process. "Right. Agreed."

"So do you think this sister has Max's tape?"

"We don't even know if there is a tape."

"You don't?"

"No."

"So what does Max have to do with this then? You think he's working with the sister?"

"We don't know that either." Then Dutch pulled out the newspaper clipping, now encased in plastic, and handed it to Gina. She began to check it out. "Allison received this clipping in the mail," Dutch told her.

"This is the write up about the plane crash that killed Elvelyn and her husband."

"Right. Crader's people have been in touch with Elvelyn's sister, this Stephanie Mitchell, and she says she never sent that clipping to Allison. And it makes sense. That clipping was sent to Allison's home, not to her office. It would seem there would be some personal knowledge for somebody to send a clipping like that to Allison's home. The sister did admit, however, that she received a phone call from a reporter who said a former White House aide had told him about the president and her sister, and did she care to comment."

"That was why those two reporters from the Associated Press and Reuters started asking you all of those questions at your press conference?"

"Right. Stephanie Mitchell must have thought that her sister was fooling with me rather than Crader, and she told those reporters so."

"Or she chose to put it out there like that," Gina suggested. "Like I said, the president cheating on the First Lady and having a child out of wedlock packs more of a punch than the vice president doing the same thing to his wife."

"Right."

"So you think Max sent Ally this clipping?" Gina asked this as she placed back on her glasses and started reading every word of the newspaper article. She was a trained attorney who practiced law for many years before she married Dutch. She knew how to sniff out clues.

"We're trying to find Max now," Dutch said as she read. "We figure he was the former White House aide who tipped off the reporters, there's no doubt in our mind about that. But the only reason we could come up with for that tip-off, and sending us that clipping, was because he has pictures or video."

Gina looked up at Dutch, a stunned look in her eyes.

"What?" he asked.

"When did you say that Vegas weekend occurred? Twelve years ago?"

"In 2000, yes. That's right. Why?"

Gina stared at her husband. "Are you sure?"

"I'm certain. It was the millennium, the year 2000. There was all of that talk about the Y2K computer bug and how the world would be plunged into chaos at the turn of the century. And we attended the congressional committee meeting in early January of that year, just after the new year. I remember it well. Why, Gina?"

"Max wanted you and Crader to see this clipping all right, but not because of any videotape of you guys having sex with a woman."

Dutch's heart began to pound. "What have you found? What is it?"

"Max wanted you to see this clipping because of the age."

Dutch frowned. "What age?"

"Elvelyn's age."

Dutch frowned. "What are you talking about?"

"Her age, Dutch! According to this article, she was twenty-eight years old when she died in that plane crash. That would mean she right around sixteen when y'all had her twelve years ago."

Dutch's heart plunged through his shoe. He snatched the article from Gina. Searched and searched and then saw it for himself. How could they have missed it? He looked back up at his wife. "*Good Lord*," he said. Looked back at her age in that article, looked back at his wife. Statutory rape, he thought. He and Crader committed statutory rape?

"How did you meet her?" Gina asked, her attorney background out in force right now.

"I didn't," Dutch said frowningly, attempting to remember that long ago weekend. "She was selected."

"Who selected her? Who set it all up?"

Dutch didn't have to even think about it. "Max," he said, it all coming together clearly now.

"Max said she was a college student he knew. Max handled the whole thing."

Gina's heart plunged too. Max Brennan was beyond a loose cannon. Max Brennan gave snakes a bad name.

"We've got to find Max," she made clear.

CHAPTER ELEVEN

The following week and Gina's birthday celebration was being held in the festively decorated Rose Garden. Many staffers and their families, along with Gina's numerous friends from Newark, were hobnobbing together to the sweet sounds of Motown. From Marvin Gaye to the Temptations to Martha and the Vandellas, every song was a delightful old school rhythm and blues.

Everybody were laughing, talking and waiting for the president and First Lady to make their appearance. LaLa and Christian were mainly hanging together, while Marcus and Sam seemed to be in deep conversation. Christian and LaLa joked that they had never seen Sam when she wasn't in deep conversation, so it didn't surprise them.

But then Crader made his appearance, and LaLa was not only surprised, but downright shocked.

Christian looked at Crader, and then looked back at LaLa.

"You're okay?" he asked her.

As Crader began to approach her, her heart began to pound. She almost looked down at her form-fitting white and yellow dress, as if to ensure she was looking her best, but she caught herself. She was done pleasing others at the expense of her own happiness. She looked fine, whether he thought so or not.

"You're okay, La?" Christian asked her again.

"Actually no," she replied.

"Want me to stay by your side?"

"Yes," she said. "Please."

And Christian stayed when Crader approached.

"Hello, Chris," he said.

"Hello, Crader."

Crader wasn't accustomed to Christian calling him by his first name, but he overlooked it. He, instead, looked at LaLa. "Hey," he said.

He looked like death warmed over, she thought. Blood-shot eyes, rumpled suit. And for what, she wondered. An hour, tops, of pleasure. "I didn't expect to see you here," she admitted.

"I know. I wasn't invited, if that's what you mean. Gina is pretty upset with me right now. But I need to talk to Dutch."

"A matter of national security?" LaLa asked, attempting to smile.

Crader looked into her mouth. He craved that bright white smile. He craved her beautiful, African lips. Her soft, sweet face. He'd give his right arm to have her and their daughter back home again. To take back what he had done. "Something like that," he replied to her.

"The president and First Lady are still getting ready in the Residence," Christian said. "Jade's with them."

Crader, however, continued to stare at LaLa. "You've been doing okay?" he asked her.

"I've been great," LaLa said, although it was hardly true.

Crader, however, saw that sparkle in her eyes he always loved, and he believed it. She was better off without him. "Good," he said, nodding his head. Regret was overwhelming him, and it felt like a knot in his throat. "I'm glad to know it."

"Yep, I'm doing just fine. I have to. I'm doing great."

"I understand you've moved back into your house in Georgetown."

"For now, yes."

LaLa would never know how painful that sounded to Crader. She had somewhere else to go. Somewhere else to stay. Something other than their life together. "I was wondering if I could get Nicole for the weekend. If that's okay with you."

LaLa nodded. "Of course it's okay with me, Crader. You're a wonderful father to our daughter."

Crader's heart squeezed when she said that. And he couldn't take it anymore. "Please come back to me," he begged, reaching for her hand.

But she snatched her hand away, causing a few people to glance over. She lowered her voice. "I told you I don't know what I'm going to do right now, Cray, I told you that."

"Okay. Okay," Crader said equally lowly, glancing around. He didn't want to make a spectacle of himself. At least, not more of a spectacle than he'd already made of himself. Especially with this new information they found out about Elvelyn. Info, if it became public, that could destroy any chance he had of taking over when Dutch's term expired.

"I didn't mean to . . .," he started. "But I respect you, La. I'll wait for you to decide. You have that right." Then he exhaled, ashamed of himself. "I need to see Dutch, so I'd better get going."

"Sure, Crader."

"Take care of yourself."

"You too."

Crader's heart was in agony, and he wanted to beg her again. But he left LaLa's side.

Christian placed his hand on LaLa's back and rubbed it. "It's okay, La," he said.

Tears began to appear in her eyes. "This was a bad idea," she said. "I shouldn't have come."

"You have to live your life, La," Christian said. "He did this to you. He's the one who has to pay. Not you."

"Thanks for your support, Christian," LaLa said with a smile that came no-where near her eyes. But she meant what she said. She was grateful for Christian's support. She even leaned against him, still in need of that support.

Dutch stood in his room-sized, walk-in closet and tore open a brand new dress shirt. He was in trousers and a t-shirt as he began putting on the shirt. Jade was also in the closet, seated on the center island.

"Didn't I tell you to get down from there?" Dutch said to her.

"You're so busy I never get a chance to spend any real time with you. You're either coming from a meeting or going to one and I hardly can say hello to you."

"Move," he said again and Jade rolled her eyes, but jumped down. She immediately grabbed the front of her father's shirt. "Let me button it. You don't let me do anything for you."

But Dutch would have none of it. He removed her hands. "I think I can button my own shirt, little girl," he said with a smile as he began walking out of the closet, buttoning his own shirt as he walked.

Jade didn't like his stubbornness, but she followed him out of the closet all the same.

"Can the president go to the movies?" she asked as they walked over to the dressing table. "I mean the real movies. Not the movie theater in the White House."

"He can go anywhere he wants to go," Dutch replied. He stood at the dressing table and combed his hair. His groomer was on call, but Dutch didn't bother to call him.

"Then take me to the movies, Daddy," Jade said with a smile.

"Get your husband to take you," Dutch replied. "Where's Christian anyway?"

"He's outside with everybody else. Where he's supposed to be."

Dutch glanced at her through the mirror. "Are you taking care of him the way you're supposed to, Jade?"

Jade hesitated. "What do you mean?"

"You know what I mean."

Jade smiled. "He's boring, Daddy."

"He's your husband."

"He's my boring husband." She moved closer to Dutch, placed her hands on his chest. "Why can't he be like you?" she asked, and Dutch looked at her. Then he removed her hands and stared at her.

"What's the matter?" she asked, surprised by that odd look in his eyes.

"What are you doing?'' Dutch asked with a frown now on his face.

"What do you mean?"

"I'm your father."

Jade laughed one of the phoniest laughs Dutch had ever heard. "I know you're my father!"

"Why are you playing games with me? Why are you *flirting* with me?"

"Flirting with you?" Jade asked, her skin blushed with shame. She never dreamed he'd call her out like this. "What are you talking about?"

"I'm your father," Dutch made clear again. "I know we didn't know each other for almost all of your life. I know I'm new to you. But you do not play the little seductress with me. Am I making myself clear, young lady?"

Jade hated when he became like this. "Yes," she said.

"You have a good man in Christian and you'd better not mess that up. I used to wonder if he was good enough for you. Kept me up nights wondering if any young man would ever be good enough for my little girl. Now I'm beginning to wonder if it's not the other way around."

Jade's heart dropped when he said that. But she didn't have time to respond. A voice was heard, a voice she hated.

"What are you two up to?" Gina's voice said airily, and they turned to the sound. She was walking into the bedroom from the adjacent dressing room entrance.

Jade, however, was already upset with her father for going there, and now this?

"Why would you say something like that?" Jade responded in her nastiest of tones, a fixed frown on her narrow face. "It's none of your business what we're up to. What kind of question is that, anyway? I'm talking to my father, okay, if that's all right with you. And it's an *A* and *B* conversation. You need to *C* your way out of it!"

Dutch looked at his daughter as if he could hardly believe her nerve, and then he slapped her hard across her face.

Jade stumbled back, grabbing the side of her now stinging face.

"Who do you think you're talking to?" Dutch asked her, his own face unable to shield his anger.

Jade held her face and stared at her father, tears forming in her eyes. "I was just telling her to stay out of my conversation," she said in a now bratty tone. "I was telling her it was none of her business."

"You don't tell her shit!" Dutch yelled. "Not like that! And my business is her business and don't you ever forget that, Jade."

Jade just stared at her father. There was anger, hurt, and embarrassment all rolled into one. He was always putting her in her place, and she was getting tired of it. And that Gina, she thought as her eyes looked angrily at Gina. She couldn't stand Gina! She was the reason. She was always the reason. There wasn't a human being she hated more than that smug-ass Gina Harber! She just knew Gina loved when Dutch slapped her. Gina just loved it, Jade would bet any amount of money. And it was too much for Jade. Too damn much. Of all the people who had to witness her humiliation. She fled from the room.

Gina looked at Dutch, amazed. Although Jade would never believe it, she actually cared about her stepdaughter. "What's wrong with her?" she asked, concern in her voice.

Dutch just stood there, upset that he laid a hand on his daughter in anger, but not regretting it, either. He exhaled. "More than we can we will ever know, I'm afraid," he said. But before he could say more, there was a knock at the door. Which was all he needed.

"Yes?" he said.

The vice president stepped inside.

"Crader?" Dutch asked, surprised.

"Sorry to disturb you."

"What is it?"

He glanced at Gina. He hadn't seen her since she met with both he and the president and explained what it all meant that they had slept with a sixteen-year old that weekend in Vegas. Because the age of consent in Vegas was sixteen, they were just legal, and just barely given Elvelyn's birthdate, which Gina also looked into. They had not committed a legal crime, she made clear, although he could tell she believed they had committed a moral one. And for Crader to have cheated on LaLa on top of that moral lapse only served to place him, he knew, at the top of Gina' shit list. A spot he also knew he rightly deserved.

Crader looked at Dutch. His old friend was still hanging in there with him, but only by a thread. But nowadays Crader would take whatever support he could get.

"What is it, Cray?" Dutch asked him again.

And Crader exhaled. Onward and upward, he thought. "We've found Max," he finally said.

Max Brennan looked at the newspaper clipping and then he looked at Crader. Crader and Dutch were seated on the sofa inside the modest home.

Max was seated in a wing chair. He had been found in Ohio, and was transported, immediately on discover, to this safe house in DC.

"It's some article, so what?" he said, tossing the clipping back to Crader. "Some female and her hubby dies. So what?"

"Ah, cut the bullshit, Max," Crader said impatiently. "It's too damn late. Did you or did you not mail that to Ally?"

Max looked at Dutch. Dutch was in a light-brown suit, his legs crossed. His intense green eyes were so focused on Max that it was making Max uncomfortable.

"Is that what you think, too, Dutch?" Max asked his former friend. "Do you think I sent some newspaper clipping to Allison?"

Dutch didn't say anything. He continued to stare at Max.

Max had a hurt look in his eyes that Dutch thought was sincere. Until Max smiled that disgusting reptilian smile of his. "So you remember her, after all?" he said. "I'm impressed."

"Why did you send it?" Crader asked.

"Admiration," Max said. "You two gentlemen, if I can use the word loosely, are so admired the world over. The President and Vice President of the United States. And neither one of you are worth a good *got*damn! Used to love and leave every woman that crossed your path. Used to bang everything that moved."

"Apparently not everything," Crader said. "We as hell never banged you."

Max moved toward Crader, causing Crader to move toward him, but Dutch pulled Crader back. "Come on guys," he said with a frown on his face. "Let's have it, Max," he then said. "What do you want?"

"Who says I want anything?"

"I don't have all night."

"No," Max said sadly. "Certainly not for the likes of me."

"What do you want, Max? I won't ask again."

Max stared at Dutch. Then he stood up. "Would you care for something to drink?" he asked.

"Oh, for crying out loud!" Crader said angrily and stood too, and began pacing.

"I'm sorry if it upsets you," Max said, "but I can't concentrate without a little pick-me-up."

"From what I hear that's all you've been doing," Crader said snidely. "Getting picked up. Or, rather, picking up young men and treating them to a night of romance in that palace of a place in Akron."

"Would you care for something to drink, Dutch?" Max asked, ignoring Crader.

Dutch had heard about it too. Max had been a closet gay for years, and although they were close friends, Dutch didn't have a clue. Or, at least, he ignored the clues and took Max at his word when he talked about loving women and wanting them.

It wasn't until he lied on Gina did their friendship end. Dutch literally kicked Max out of the White House when he falsely accused Gina of unfaithfulness.

"No, Max," he said. "I don't want anything to drink."

Max expected as much. But that wasn't going to stop him from getting his kick on. Dutch ruined his political career when he fired him. He had had hopes of running for office himself, maybe even becoming a governor someday. Now nobody would return his phone calls. Not even the young, eager White House staffers he used to supervise.

He walked behind the sizeable bar and poured himself a glass of champagne. Crader looked at Dutch, as if to get permission to kick Max's ass and be done with it, but Dutch's expression gave him no clues.

"I feel like celebrating," Max said as he returned to his seat. "My old friend is in my presence-although Secret Service agents surreptitiously surround this presence, but still. My old friend has paid me a visit. I feel honored."

"Enough of this shit," Crader said. "We didn't come here to play games with you!"

"Who's playing games?" Max asked.

"Where are the photographs, Max?" Dutch asked.

Max looked at him. "What photographs?"

Dutch stared at him.

"I don't have any photographs."

"Sure about that?" Crader asked.

Max hesitated. "I'm positive."

"Then what the fuck are these?" Crader asked as he threw a small stack of photographs, with thumbnail negatives, onto the coffee table. The photos were obviously of two men and a female, all three having sex.

Max picked up the photos. Closer inspection showed Dutch, Crader, and Elvelyn having sex. Max was astounded. He looked at Crader. "Where did you get these?"

"Surprised, are you? Ready to talk now? Who do you think you're dealing with, boy? You sold them, we bought them. The people you sold these to, they came to us with their own price. You know why? Because everybody has a price. And one thing's for damn sure: your offer will never be higher than ours."

Max swallowed hard.

"Where's the rest of the photographs, Max?" Dutch asked.

"That's all of them."

"The negatives?"

"That's it, right there," Max said, pointing to the negatives on the table. "There are no more."

"Are you the person who tipped off that Associated Press reporter?"

About Vegas, yes. I told them to ask about Vegas. I don't know what they were talking about with that eight month old child business. I don't know anything about that."

Crader already knew the sister was behind that part of the rumor.

Dutch stood up. "You'll regret it, Max," he said, "if you're lying."

"I'm not lying! That's it. That's all. Why would I lie?"

Dutch stood up. He placed his hands in his pants pockets and continued to stare at Max.

"What?" Max asked, irritated by his stare.

"Did you know that girl was sixteen?"

Max paused, and then smiled. "Of course I knew. You could have known it too, but neither one of you bothered to ask. Y'all just didn't care."

Dutch could feel a sense of moral decay. Because even Max was right sometimes. He just didn't care back then. He wanted pleasure and she was there to pleasure him. That poor child. What kind of man would have done what he did?

Max knew Dutch. He could see that regret, that anguish, in those big-ass green eyes of his. And he pounced.

"One day," Max said to Dutch, "will be your reckoning day. One day all of the shit you've pulled on people, all of the pain you've caused folks to go through, is going to come back on you. All of it! One day, Walter Harber, you're going to fall on your knees and beg forgiveness. And then you'll see what it's like to be the one left behind. Then you'll see what it's like to be the one with his back against the wall, and there's no way out." Tears suddenly appeared in Max's eyes. "One day, Walter Harber, you'll have your reckoning day."

Dutch stared at his former friend. And for a moment, a brief, ephemeral moment, Dutch felt like a fraud. He'd done more than his share of bad things in this life, but somehow he managed to believe that he was one of the good guys in the end. But now, for this one moment, as he stared in the eyes of a man he used to love, he saw the other man inside of him. And he couldn't find anything good about that man; about *that* Dutch Harber.

It spooked him. For a moment. But he quickly recovered. This was Max lecturing him. Snake-in-the-grass Max. He'd be out of his mind to let a prick like that get to him.

"Take your time, Cray," he said. But he hesitated again, with that troubled look still in his eyes, and continued to stare at his former friend. Who did he think he was telling Dutch Harber about a reckoning day? After all the shit he'd pulled on people he had the nerve to tell Dutch about a reckoning day? It was hypocrisy in the extreme, Dutch thought, as he looked once more at Max, and then left the building.

Crader, who never liked Max Brennan, walked over to Max.

"Why are you still here?" Max asked nervously as Crader began moving toward him. "I told you there are no more photos."

"What about videos?" Crader asked.

"There are no videos!" Max insisted. "What are you talking about?"

"I don't know if I believe you." Crader was now standing in front of Max.

"That's your problem," Max said, standing up.

As soon as he stood, Crader grabbed him, moved behind him, and placed his arm around his neck. He then pulled out a gun and as Max fought hard and protested, he placed the barrel of that gun deep inside of Max's mouth. Max's eyes popped wide, and all of his movements ceased.

"The day a photograph, a videotape, or anything related to that Vegas weekend becomes public," Crader said, "will not be your reckoning day. No, sir. To hell with reckoning. Because the day any of those items appear anywhere in public, will be the day that you die."

He tightened his grip on Max. Max began to sweat. "Just one release, Max," Crader continued, "and you will leave this earth. I don't care if you knew about it. I don't care if you didn't know about it. I don't care if you were in the hospital in traction when that one photograph inadvertently was made public. If it goes public, you go dead. Are you getting the message here, Mr. Brennan?"

Max nodded carefully, to avoid any accidental firing, as sweat beads appeared on his forehead.

Then Crader pulled the weapon out of Max's mouth and released him. As soon as he did, Max collapsed in relief to the floor.

And Crader, eventually, after having the boys come in and work Max over just enough to keep him honest, left him collapsed on that floor.

CHAPTER TWELVE

Marcus slammed Jade against the back wall of the basement and began to fuck her vigorously. He had already lifted up her shirt, revealing taut breasts that he ravaged with his mouth. He had already slung down her skirt and panties, revealing an already moist mound that he slid her slightly up the wall and ravaged with his tongue. Now he had his own pants around his ankles and was ramming his cock into her pussy as if there was no tomorrow. And the way he felt tonight, he didn't give a damn if there wasn't.

And it was all that *got*damn Dutch Harber's fault, he thought angrily as he fucked Dutch's daughter. That smug sonafabitch Dutch Harber! First he didn't show up for his own wife's birthday party until the party was almost over, which showed how little he cared about that wife of his. Then he had all of this attitude. Telling Marcus what the deal was like he was his damn daddy. It was time for him to make a decision, Dutch told him tonight. He couldn't remain at Jade and Christian's house much longer. And that bastard told him that, not just in front of Gina, but in front of Christian, too. And in front of Sam, who was about as ditsy as they came.

Jade began to moan in pleasure as he fucked her, and Marcus angrily covered her mouth. "That husband and mother of yours are upstairs, remember?" her reminded her angrily.

But Jade needed no reminding because she didn't care, either. The way Dutch was always defending Gina was beginning to grate on her mightily. And the way he slapped her tonight. Just slapped her for absolutely no reason at all. Gina had to go, she thought as Marcus slammed into her so hard, with such dick force, that she was in physical pain. If it was the last thing she did, she was going to make sure that Marcus's plan, bankrolled by Thurston Osgood, worked. The way Marcus explained it to her, Thurston Osgood was ready to bite. Thurston, Marcus had told Jade, was convinced that Dutch loved Gina so much that hurting Gina would be the worse punishment anybody could put on Dutch. Worse, they believed, than anything they could ever do to Dutch himself.

But Jade knew better. Yes, Dutch might cry for a minute if something happened to Gina. He might be hurt for a second. But he'd get over it. And then her mother could claim him, and he would be theirs and theirs alone. No Gina. No more Gina. And, if Jade was to completely have her way, no fat-faced Little Walt, either.

That was why she inwardly screamed in pleasure as Marcus hammered her mercilessly with his dick. Marcus was thinking about Dutch and Gina too, as he fucked Jade, as his own dick was getting sore from the pounding he was putting on

Dutch's little girl. Only his thoughts weren't at all about getting rid of Gina, but what he could do to really get Dutch. Because he was going to get him. And he was going to make it count.

He was so caught up in imagining the fall of Dutch Harber, and pounding the shit out of Dutch Harber's child, that he didn't realize they had company until he was just on the brink of release. He glanced over and saw Sam standing there. Jade couldn't see her, but he could.

And Sam was aghast. "Oh, *really* now!" she said in that loud, high-pitched voice that caused Jade to nearly die where she stood when she heard her mother's voice. Jade immediately pushed Marcus away from her with a violent shove. Marcus's engorged dick slipped out of her when she pushed him, and it slung cum all over her as soon as it slipped out.

But that wasn't the only jolt. Because coming up behind Sam, too stunned to speak, was Christian.

They sat Indian-style in the middle of their big, welcoming bed. Dutch was in command and Gina was seated on his lap, facing him. He was kissing her, long and hard, and she was returning the favor. His hand gently rubbed her bouncy, soft hair and her fingers raked through his jet-black, silky hair. They were both naked and in need of a release. His tanned body was rock hard, from his thick chest and muscular biceps, to his ripped abs and fully erect penis, and her body was soft, dark brown, and toned, from her taut breasts to her flat stomach, to her small arms encircling his neck. They were putting the night behind them and determined to enjoy every inch of her birthday.

Dutch then took his kisses downward, to Gina's more-than-ready breasts. She loved the way his entire mouth covered her in a wide suction that not only hardened her nipples even more, but caused sensations to course through her entire breast. He went from one breast to the other one, taking in deep, full sucks. He was enjoying his wife with the ease of a man who wasn't about to rush this delight.

Gina wasn't rushing it, either. She leaned her head back and thrust her breasts to him, giving him full access. And he took it. He took it repeatedly.

And then he gently laid her down on the bed, her head touching the middle pillow, as he moved his kisses down her body until he was at one of his favorite spots. Gina adored the way he licked her clit in wide sweeps. None of those quick bites that gave quick sensations.

Dutch, instead, moved slowly, his pink tongue covering the entire lower end of her pink vagina and then carefully sliding between the folds as his mouth swept up to her clit. Over and over he did this slow motion fuck, causing her body to wrench into a kind of pulsating elation.

"You like it, baby?" he asked her as he kept kissing, sucking, licking her.

"Yes. I love it. Don't know if I can bear it."

"You can bear it," Dutch shot back. "I know my baby can bear anything I do to her pussy." He said this and did more to her pussy, as he began kissing her deeper into her folds.

"Oh, Dutch!" she cried out, her face displaying the intensity she felt. "I can't take it!"

"That's what you do," Dutch cried back. "You scream my name! You let me know you love what I do to you!"

"Oh, Dutch, I love it. I love it too much!"

As her pulsating became high body arching, Dutch put his fingers inside of her vagina while he sucked her clit in kisses so hard that Gina felt as if she could lose control at any moment. She arched against him and arched against him harder. He wiggled her clit and fingered her, faster and faster. Gina closed her legs around his head, entrapping him in her pussy. But instead of her clenching movements causing him to let up, he went all out, fingering her harder and kissing her deeper.

She screamed so hard and arched so high that he knew he had to let up, before agents broke down their bedroom door to ensure they weren't under attack.

Gina took the lull in his frenetic mouth fuck to do a little mouth fucking of her own. She moved onto her knees and laid him down, his gorgeous hair flapping over his forehead as his head hit the pillow. She moved to his midsection and began sucking his dick. She sucked long and hard, her ass in the air, and Dutch placed his hand on that ass, massaging her in squeezes as he enjoyed the wonderment that was her tongue.

But if she thought for a moment that her pleasuring him would give her pussy a rest, she was mistaken. Dutch was already missing the feel of her soaking wet folds as he fingered her again. He could hardly wait to get his dick inside of that. He could hardly wait until her wetness and his wetness intermingled for what he knew was going to be a rousing cum.

But he already felt intermingled with her. He loved how her tongue on his dick and his finger in her pussy somehow felt connected. He felt sensation in his penis that rippled through his body like a current, and jangled through his hand, creating that connection.

"That's right, baby," he said as her mouth went all the way down on his rod. "That's what I want. That's it. That's it. That's it, baby, that's it!"

And then it was too much for even Dutch to bear. He remained where he lay as he lifted Gina on top of him, her face to his face. When he finally slid inside of her, when he finally penetrated that warm inner sanctum of the woman he loved, his cock began to feel like a vibrator inside of her.

At first he didn't move. He rested his penis in those sweet folds and stared at this woman he had on his hands. He touched her cheeks, stared into her eyes. He'd had so many females in his life, so many up and down the coast. And it was all just a game to him, just a warm-up act for this real affection, this true love he felt for Gina.

Sometimes he wondered why. What was it about Regina that made him decide that she was the one above all others? She wasn't the smartest woman he'd ever met. Sam would take that prize easily. She wasn't the prettiest woman, either. And goodness knows he couldn't begin to count the many arguments and disagreements they'd had in the course of their marriage.

But it was Gina who wasn't about to let him have his cake and eat it too. It was Gina who made him understand that he was going to be with her, and her alone, or they weren't going to be together. All of his previous girlfriends would have forgiven him anything, and often did. Would let him get away with everything.

But he knew, with Gina, he had to bring his *A* game. She wasn't putting up with his bullshit, period, end of story. That was a fact. And if he acted right she would be in his corner, period, end of story. That was another fact. And Dutch Harber was smart enough to know that Regina Harber was exactly the kind of woman he needed in his corner. In his life. Period. End of story.

And as he began to move inside of her, with the tightening of her folds around his cock coming almost immediately, he couldn't imagine living without this woman in his life. He held her beautiful brown face in his hands, kissed her on the nose, pulled her down against his body, and fucked her.

He wrapped his arms around her in a tight embrace as he thrashed into her, faster and faster, his mouth gaping open in a kind of enchanted intensity as he fucked her.

"*Gi-naaa!*" he screamed in a pained tone as they screwed, and she called his name, too, because she knew what he meant. Her ass was shaking from his thrashings and shaking at a dizzying pace. And her pussy was throbbing with the roaring sensations.

Dutch was throbbing too, as his gyrations continued to increase; as the feeling of love for Gina continued to make him hold her tightly against his rock-hard body. He felt every inch of her as he slid in and almost out of her repeatedly. He was no stranger to the sensations of a female's cunt, but this was one pussy he could never tire of. Because Gina knew how to tighten around him. She knew how to let him take the lead, to not attempt to match him thrash for thrash, until the exact right moment.

Which, she instinctively knew, was right now.

As he spilled out into her, she took in his release by taking over his movements. It was Gina, now, that was taking the lead, sliding her body up and down on his throbbing penis, increasing his throbs and increasing her own, until even she couldn't move. Until her body, too, was clenching in the euphoria of cum.

It was such a vaulted cum that their throbbing didn't stop for minutes on end. And even after all of the pulsating finally ceased, they still couldn't move.

It would be several more minutes of just lying there, breathing hard and heavy and eventually with normal regulation, did either of them finally speak.

"I take it you saw Max tonight," she said. He had immediately immersed himself into the party after his meeting with Max, and didn't have a private moment to tell her anything.

"I saw him."

"Did he admit to knowing about that newspaper clipping, and those photographs?"

"He admitted it. Claims there are no more, and no video."

"You believe him?"

"We'll see."

"With friends like him," Gina said with a shake of her head. "He probably thought he was setting you up for a statutory rape charge. And he would have been, Dutch, except for the fact that the age of consent in Vegas is sixteen. But I doubt if Max knew that at the time."

"I doubt it too," Dutch said, sadly. "It was a set up."

"Some friend," Gina said again. Then she looked at Dutch. "Do you consider the matter resolved?"

Dutch exhaled. "Inasmuch as it can be with a snake like Max. We'll see," was the best he could say about it.

Gina looked at Dutch. He seemed satisfied, if not completely triumphant, but she still felt uneasy. As if more was brewing. As if that calm, normal life she had been praying for ever since she married Dutch Harber, was slowly but decidedly slipping further and further away.

CHAPTER THIRTEEN

Dutch Harber, in his tailored Italian silk suit, entered the West Wing the next morning feeling better than he had in weeks. The situation with Max might not be resolved in the long run, but at least it didn't blow up in their faces. Besides, Max was no fool. Crader had already made clear what would happen to him if he crossed the president. If there were more pictures in his possession, or some videotape somewhere, he had enough moxie to keep it under wraps. So, in Dutch's mind, that catastrophe at least seemed averted for now.

But as was becoming the norm for his life in Washington, however, another catastrophe met Dutch just outside of the Oval Office when he walked up and saw his son-in-law lying prone on the bench. He still wore his suit from last night's birthday celebration, and his blond hair, which was usually pristine, was a spiky, hot mess.

"Christian?" Dutch said aloud, causing Christian to jump and then open his eyes. When he saw the president standing there, his briefcase in hand, ready to get to work, he quickly sat up. And then stood up.

"Mr. President, sir," he said nervously, raking his hair in place. "Good morning."

Dutch, however, was frowning. "What are you doing here?"

"I was. . ." He just stared at Dutch, his blue eyes troubled.

Dutch looked around. It was early, but the West Wing was beginning to come alive again. He began heading for the entrance into the Oval. "Come with me," he ordered the young man.

Christian followed Dutch into the Oval Office, waited in front of the desk as Dutch walked around to his seat behind the desk. Dutch flipped through some documents on that desk that were already awaiting his perusal, and then he sat down. When he sat down, Christian sat down, too.

"What happened?" Dutch asked him.

Sex happened, Christian thought, as he recounted to Dutch what he witnessed after returning home from Gina's birthday bash. He had work to do in his study, so that was where he ended up. When he began hearing noises downstairs, slapping noises, he headed toward the basement. Sam, apparently, had heard the same noises because she was already down there.

And they both saw it.

"Saw what?" Dutch asked. He was leaned back in his swivel chair, his hand under his chin, rubbing it, as he stared at his son-in-law.

"We saw Jade and Marcus," Christian said, his face distressed. "Making out."

Dutch frowned. "Making out? They were fucking?"

Christian swallowed hard. It wasn't exactly the word he would have chosen. But it was exactly the right word. "Yes, sir," he said.

It wasn't as if it was unexpected, Dutch wanted to tell the young man. But he didn't go there yet. "How did you go from catching Jade 'making out' with Marcus, to sleeping outside my office?"

Christian let out a harsh exhale. "I went for Marcus, and pushed him away from my wife. And we started fighting."

It was no contest, Dutch knew. Marcus probably beat his ass.

"It was kind of a one-sided fight," Christian admitted. "But Sam tried to help me, and Jade made Marcus back off. I then told Marcus he had to get out of my house, but Jade said that you had bought the house for her, not for both of us, and if anybody was leaving it was going to be me."

"Jade said that?"

"Yes, sir. She even got into it with her mother over Marcus. It was a terrible argument, sir, just terrible. And Miss Redding said if Marcus didn't leave tonight, she was leaving tonight. Jade didn't say anything. And Miss Redding packed her bags, called a cab, and left."

This surprised Dutch. "Where did she go?"

"Probably caught a plane back to South Carolina the way she packed up everything like that. But I didn't ask. I was still getting into it with Jade. She was trying to claim that it wasn't what we thought it was and if I was a better husband to her she wouldn't be in some basement with another man to begin with. She was talking crazy, sir. She was blaming me for her own wrongdoing. And she meant it, too. She went on and on about it. She said you weren't there for her when she was growing up, and her mother didn't treat her with any kind of affection, and she was playing the victim like nobody's business. I was amazed. It didn't even sound like Jade."

But Dutch wasn't amazed. Not by a long shot. He picked up his phone, requested a secure outside line, and phoned Jade's cell. It took forever, but it was finally answered. By Marcus.

"Hello?"

Dutch's jaw tightened. "Good morning, Marcus," he said, prompting Christian to move around in his seat. "Let me speak to my daughter."

"She's asleep."

"Then wake her up."

There was resistance to his order, Dutch could tell that, but eventually Jade came onto the line.

"Hello?"

"Good morning. This is your father."

"Hey, Daddy."

"I want to see you here, at the White House."

"When?"

"Now, Jade."

Jade hesitated. "Christian's been talking to you, hasn't he?"

"I've got to be on Capitol Hill by ten this morning, so I need you over here so we can talk before I leave."

"But I'm not even up yet."

"Then get up, and get over here." Then he thought about it. "And bring Marcus with you," he added, and hung up the phone.

What was he going to do with that daughter of his, he wondered.

But he didn't wonder long. He phoned Ralph Shaheen, head of the Secret Service, and asked if he could find out from his men if they knew where that cab took Sam Redding. He received the answer back within minutes.

She was actually still in town, Ralph said, and had checked into the Watergate Hotel.

Which was a fitting location, Dutch thought, considering this family of his.

They waited in the Residence as if they were waiting on a death row execution. Solemn was the word. Jade and Marcus sat side by side on the sofa, and Sam sat alone, in the flanking chair. It took all she had to even be there after the way Jade treated her last night. But Dutch had phoned and had insisted.

"You should have seen her, Dutch," Sam had said to him when he phoned her. "She behaved as if Marcus Rance meant the world to her, and the rest of us could go to hell. She's never been so disrespectful in all her life."

"She's a troubled young lady," Dutch said.

"What are we going to do?"

"I've spoken to her about therapy, but she's told me a flat no. But I may have to take matters into my own hand."

"Good luck with that," Sam had told him. "You should have seen her last night. I don't know what happened at that party, but something snapped in our daughter. And it changed her."

Dutch had slapped her, that was what snapped, he thought. And she had already changed long before last night. Sam was just blind to the full import of the change.

"I'm sending a car to get you," he said. "I need to find out what can be done, if anything, to salvage this situation."

And only for Dutch did she agree.

He had already agreed to pay off her debts. That was already in the works. And not just some of her debts, either. All of them. When he told her, she jumped for joy. She thanked him, and she thanked Gina, too. Jade could say whatever she wanted about Gina Harber, but Sam didn't see her as anything but an ally.

And if there was a better man out there than Dutch, Sam had yet to meet him. He was a true friend indeed. A man whose largess had allowed her to keep her business afloat and her home as well. Paid for in full. That was Dutch Harber.

And although she knew Dutch would have helped her whether Gina approved or not, she was pleased to know that Gina approved. That kept the stress away. And the idea that she could have stolen that woman's husband away from her just by showing more cleavage and batting her big eyes was even more ridiculous to her now than it was when Sam first broached the subject. A man like Dutch, she believed, was too ethical to stray that easily.

As soon as the doors to the West Sitting Hall opened, everybody sat up at attention. But it wasn't the president arriving. It was Gina.

"Good morning, everybody," Gina said as she entered. She was dressed conservatively, in a white and brown cardigan sweater and skirt set, and Sam was impressed with her style. This would be the woman Wham Bam Harber would eventually settle down and marry, and it was no surprise to Sam that she would be a smart, savvy sister. Dutch, she'd inwardly suspected, always favored the sistas.

Gina offered everyone drinks, everyone declined, and then she sat on the second sofa in the room, the one facing Jade and Marcus.

"The president had to take a critical call from the German Chancellor, but he'll be here momentarily."

"Okay, you told us, so you can leave now," Jade said to Gina.

Marcus looked at Jade, astounded. Or, at least, he was playing the role of a man astounded. "Don't be rude," he said to her. "That's my sister you're talking to." He knew he had to keep Gina in his corner. He lose Gina, he lose access. He lose access, he could kiss his plan and all of those millions Thurston Osgood had been floating under his nose goodbye.

Gina, however, just sat there. She was accustomed to Jade's little comments. They didn't bother her. Besides, Gina thought with an inward smile, Dutch had taken care of her little sassy butt last night, and on Gina's birthday. A kind of ironic birthday gift.

"So, sis," Marcus said smilingly, as if, Gina thought, he had nothing to do with why this emergency meeting was being called in the first place, "when are we going to hook up again at Bridge Gap?"

"I'll have to check my schedule," she said.

"I haven't heard a word from the director about that job they offered me. Board approval shouldn't take this long."

"It shouldn't, but I'm sure she'll let you know. You have to be patient in DC."

Marcus didn't like the way she phrased that, but he continued to smile nonetheless. He wasn't blowing this chance. He had already contacted his crew. Everything was already set up and waiting for that perfect time.

It would take only a few minutes longer before the doors to the West Sitting Hall were opened again, and Dutch and Christian came through. Jade was a little uncomfortable seeing Christian with her father, but she played it off.

Dutch spoke and sat beside Gina. Christian spoke to Sam only, and sat beside Dutch. It was as if the lots had been cast, and the sides had already been taken.

Dutch, however, didn't have time to play games or to beat around any bushes. He had to be on Capitol Hill soon enough and he needed to take a break before he left. This little get together was not his idea of a break.

"Did you allow Marcus Rance to have sex with you last night?" he asked his daughter point blank.

Gina looked at Marcus and Jade, anger in her eyes.

Jade decided to deflect. "You don't know what it's like, Daddy," she said. "Christian acts all innocent around you, but you just don't know."

"So it's my fault?" Christian said.

"If you were the kind of husband you're supposed to be," Jade answered, "nothing would have happened. And nothing happened anyway! Don't believe that nonsense Christian's telling you."

"It isn't nonsense," Sam spoke up and said.

Everybody looked at her.

"Stay out of it, Ma," Jade said.

Sam looked at Dutch. "In answer to your question, yes, Dutch, your daughter, our daughter, is one fucked up individual who allowed this man to hold her against a wall and do all sorts of sexual things to her." Then Sam looked at Jade. "And it wasn't the first time, either."

Christian was surprised by this. Dutch wasn't.

"I never caught them before," Sam made clear, "but I sure as hell suspected it."

"Well, we can't help your suspicions," Marcus said with a smile on his face.

"But you had sex with her last night," Christian said to Marcus. "That wasn't a suspicion. That was a fact."

"In your mind," Marcus said, continuing to smile. "Not in my mind."

"Then something's wrong with your mind because I know what I saw with my own two eyes." Dutch looked at Christian. It was about time, he thought. "And it wasn't an illusion what I saw last night. It was you pounding into my wife, not an illusion."

"Whatever, Chris," Marcus said dismissively, which only inflamed Christian's passion.

"I trusted you!" Christian screamed. "I invited you into my home. I tried to be a friend to you! And this is how you repay me?"

"I don't owe you shit!" Marcus yelled, forgetting to smile. "Jade helped me out. And nobody else!"

"Jade is my wife," Christian reminded him. "We're one in the same."

Jade looked at Christian. Dutch stared at her. "One in the same?" she said to her husband. "We aren't one in the same, what are you talking about? You disgust me. All you want to do is work, work, work. You don't even know how to have any fun. You're nothing like me!"

"You used to think we had a lot in common."

"Well, I thought wrong, didn't I?"

"What are you doing?" Christian asked, tears coming into his eyes. "How can you talk like this? I love you and you know it."

"Stop saying that!"

"But it's true, Jade."

"Then that sounds like a personal problem to me." Her face was frowned. "You disgust me, I abhor you, and you're talking about love?"

Dutch leaned forward. Gina could see that he had had it with that daughter of his. "Marcus," he said, "I want you to go back to the house, pack up your bags, and leave my daughter's residence."

But Jade was horrified. "That's my house," she told her father. "You can't control my house just because you paid for it. The title is in my name now. Mine. And Marcus is staying with me!"

Dutch stared at his daughter. It felt like a game of chess to Gina. "Are you telling me, are you telling your husband, that you're choosing Marcus over him? That you no longer wish to remain in your marriage?"

Christian's heart was pounding as he waited for Jade's response. Jade seemed hesitant too, it seemed to Gina, but she pressed on.

"That's exactly what I'm telling you," she said to Dutch.

Christian's heart plunged. He stared at his wife for a long time. He wiped his tears away but kept staring at her. He thought they could overcome many things. Even last night. Now he knew better.

He got up, and headed out of the room.

"Christian, wait!" Gina yelled after him, but he kept on walking. For his own self-respect, he kept on walking.

Dutch leaned back. Even he didn't see this coming.

It was Sam who spoke up through the long silence. "I'm taking Jade back to South Carolina with me," she said.

Jade stared at her with horror in her eyes. Marcus stared too. He needed Jade to execute his plan. No Jade, no plan.

"I'm a grown woman," Jade said. "I'm not going back there."

"Yes, you are," Sam said without hesitation. "I'm not Christian. And you don't have me wrapped around your finger the way you do your father. I dare you to buck me."

It all flooded back for Jade. The lack of warmth. The lack of consideration. The way her mother's word was supreme and she would knock the fire out of her if she didn't obey. She lived in pure terror of her mother back then. And even to this day, if her mother, like now, put her foot down firmly enough, she still lived in pure terror of her mother. It was irrational and it was unreasonable. But Dutch and Gina did notice how Jade didn't dispute her mother's contention, nor did she say another word.

LaLa had just stepped out of the shower inside her Georgetown home, and was drying off when the doorbell rang.

"Great," she said aloud as she removed her shower cap. She wrapped the towel around her body, knotting it just above her breasts, and hurried to the front door. It more than likely was one of her aides bringing over the draft copy of the speech she was set to deliver tomorrow at the women's center. But when she looked through the peephole and saw Christian rather than an aide, she quickly opened up.

"Christian," she said, urging him inside. The agent in charge of her protection remained on the home's porch as Christian entered, and she closed the door behind him.

"What's wrong?" she asked him.

Christian kept shaking his blond head, fighting back tears.

LaLa could just feel his pain. "Come on, bud," she said as she moved him toward the sofa. "Let's have a sit down."

They sat on the sofa, side by side.

"Now tell me what's going on."

"I'm so sorry to bother you, La. I didn't mean to come here and bother you like this."

"Will you stop! What's happened, Chris? Is it Jade?"

Christian nodded his head. "The President made her come to the White House, and to bring Marcus. The things she said, La. I was amazed."

"What things?"

"About our marriage. About me. She prefers Marcus over me."

"Marcus?" LaLa was astounded. "Jade and Marcus?"

Christian nodded, looked at LaLa. "Yeah. I caught, me and Miss Redding, we caught Jade and Marcus making out. Fucking!" he said angrily. It was a word he'd never used before, but the president had described it correctly. "And then it's like she blames me. She says she doesn't want our marriage, La. She doesn't want us to be together anymore. She says I disgust her."

"Oh, Chris," LaLa said and pulled him into her arms. He grabbed hold of her, tightly, and almost sobbed in her arms. It hurt just that badly.

But he refused to cry. It seemed useless to cry over somebody who said he disgusted her. So he tried with all he had to forget about Jade, as he sat on that sofa with LaLa.

And LaLa was patient with him. She knew what he was going through. She held him, rubbed his hair, comforted him. But the more she held him the more he began to realize that he was right where he wanted to be: in LaLa's arms. He experienced her. He experienced her sweet perfume scent, and her kindness, and her heart, and her integrity, and he couldn't cry anymore.

Because, in truth, there was rarely a time that he made love to Jade when he wasn't wishing, just a little, that it was LaLa's vagina he was shoving into. LaLa, he knew, would have never betrayed him.

He moved back, to look into her compassionate eyes, and he was even more certain. He wanted her. He *needed* her. He looked down, at her sultry lips, and then he knew. He knew. He moved closer. LaLa backed up slightly. But he kept coming.

LaLa wanted to back up again. What was he doing? They couldn't go there, what did he think he was doing? But it was Christian doing it. Sweet, wonderful Christian. And her feelings for her friend, for his pain and agony, wouldn't let her back away.

Besides, she thought as he kept coming closer, those luscious red lips of his were just too damned sexy for her to even pretend to ignore. They were friends. What was a little kiss between friends?

Only it wasn't a little kiss. There, in fact, was nothing little about it. Christian came in with a smooch that pressed so hard against LaLa's lips she thought he was stinging her.

"Open your mouth, La," he said. "I need to taste you."

LaLa thought to keep it closed. They had no business doing this! But Christian's lips kept nudging, his voice kept urging, so she opened. She opened her mouth and allowed Christian in.

And that movement alone opened the floodgates of passion. All restraints, all thoughts of restraining, were gone. They were, at that moment in time, all in.

Christian unknotted LaLa's towel and moved his lips from her mouth to her freshly scrubbed breasts. He moved in such a fluid motion. He kissed them, fondled them, and sucked them. Then he rubbed his lips against them in a powerful tease that caused LaLa to grab his head and bury his face into her sizeable breasts.

And Christian feasted on them. Jade was so skinny, practically a flat-chested wench compared to LaLa. LaLa was all woman. Big and full and oh so gorgeous to Christian. He couldn't get enough of her. All thoughts of Jade and what she did to him were gone, when he sucked on LaLa's breasts.

He opened her legs as he sucked her and began to finger her clit. It was a trick he learned from the president. One day he stopped in to holler at Little Walt and walked casually into the Treaty Room, expecting it to be empty. He had hoped to grab a seat and finish the last of his speech corrections for Gina. And there was the president, with Gina on his lap, sucking on her half-exposed breast and fingering her clit at the same time. They were newly married at the time, and Christian wasn't all that experienced, but he saw enough to know that Gina could not have been more pleased. He quickly stepped back out, before he was detected, but he never forgot that scene.

Gina was screaming in pleasure as Dutch finger-fucked her. Now Christian had LaLa screaming too.

But he wanted more. Kissing and sucking were fine, but he wanted to make his fantasy come true. He unzipped and pulled down his pants as he sucked and fingered her. His long dick sprang out stiff and hard as soon as his briefs slid down. And he didn't waste another second. He was on top of LaLa, lying her down. He put his dick into her vagina without even thinking about protection. He had to feel her raw.

He felt her pussy on his dick in a contact that was nothing short of pure electricity. They sizzled together as he stroked her. And LaLa stroked back, matching him. Her legs were wrapped around his back and he was pumping deep inside of her. She could not believe this was happening, that she was actually being fucked by Christian. But it was true. Christian was pushing deeper and deeper into her, making wonderful love to her, making her feel like the most important woman in the world to him. Nothing else mattered. Nobody else mattered.

Until they came, together, in a wave of vibration and ecstasy. Christian cried out as the feelings had his dick throbbing in release, and LaLa cried out, too.

And then she realized, as soon as the flow of released began to ebb, that it did matter. She was a married woman, regardless of what they were going through. And he was a married man.

And she also realized, like a jolt, that she had just done exactly what she always said she'd never do. She's just done with Christian what Crader had done with Elvelyn. She'd just done to Crader what Crader had done to her!

And so easily she had done it.

The truth of it staggered her.

CHAPTER FOURTEEN

Marcus, Sam, and Jade arrived back at Jade's house. Marcus made his way down into the basement, certain that Jade would soon follow. But first he had to get ready. He smuggled in the gun days ago, when the Secret Service was accompanying Jade and Sam on some shopping excursion they made together. Jade was the president's daughter and therefore entitled to Secret Service protection. Marcus was the First Lady's half-brother and was not entitled, he was glad to know for this purpose, to squat.

He therefore could go and come with impunity, as he often did. As he did the day they went on their shopping spree.

He got into the car Gina had purchased for him when he was first released, a car he kept parked on the street in front of Jade's home, and made his way to the Osgood Mansion. He got the idea on how it all could work the night Jade phoned the president about her mother acting a fool, and the president came rushing right over. Marcus had expected Dutch to have the Secret Service agent enter the home and check on Sam, not come over himself. That, Marcus thought, would be the quick and easy way to do it.

But Dutch didn't roll like that. He came himself. He had just come back in town from

Finland, had to be dead tired, but he came himself. Marcus now knew why. It was the same reason he called them to the White House this morning. Dutch Harber did not allow anyone, not even the Secret Service, to get involved with his personal family business. The way Marcus saw it Dutch was too arrogant and prideful to even consider allowing someone else to handle it. He always handled it himself. Always.

Marcus was counting on that pride this day. He was counting on Dutch handling personal family affairs himself, to help him to accomplish his goal now, and make his dreams come true.

Marcus met, the day he was given the gun, with Thurston Osgood. He also saw, once more, Henry Osgood seated like lifeless furniture in his wheelchair. Thurston had experts there, his people, who provided Marcus with details on exactly what he had to do. Marcus was then given the gun and all of the accessories. He also received instructions on where the money drop would occur once it was reported, in the media, that the task had been accomplished and the president was dead.

Marcus returned home and began his preparations. He knew this scheme was fraught with risk. What if the president didn't show up? What if Sam tried some maneuver? She was certainly smart enough to outsmart him. What if Jade figured something out? What if the president had a tail on him wherever he went that he didn't even know about? It was fraught with risk. But the money, the freedom, that old-fashioned thing called revenge, made it all worth the risk to Marcus.

So he waited for the right time. Day in and day out he waited. Until this morning, at the White House, when all of this talk of Sam taking Jade back to South Carolina, and Dutch attempting to kick him out of Jade's house too, and Christian catching them doing their thing last night. He knew then, after all of those factors, that today was that right time.

Now he was waiting again. He had a tote bag at his feet, and it was filled with everything he would need. And he waited for Jade to make her appearance.

He didn't have long to wait. Because sure enough, the door upstairs opened, footsteps were heard on the basement steps, and there was an appearance. Only it wasn't Jade. It was Sam. And already, he thought, his plan had hit a snag.

He had expected to handle Jade first, so that she could place the phone call, and then quickly go upstairs and deal with Sam. But now he had to improvise.

He was seated in the living room area of the apartment-like basement when Sam made her appearance. He smiled. He knew better than most how to turn on the charm.

"Well, hello there, Miss Redding. What can I do you for?"

"We're leaving in the morning," Sam said with no thought of small talk with him. Marcus used to view it as a slight, as some level of disrespect. But over time, after being around her more, he came to realize she was just being Sam. She was blunt with everybody.

"Yeah, I remember you mentioned something about taking Jade back to South Carolina."

"When do you plan to get out of here?"

Marcus wanted to snap back. *Who does this bitch think she's talking to*, he thought. But he smiled instead. "I'll be out of here today, matter of fact," he said, rising to his feet. "I just need to get your opinion." He unzipped his tote bag.

"My opinion?" Sam asked. "On what?"

"On this job offer I've been given," he said as he stood up. "The contract is kind of elaborate. I was hoping you'd take a look at it for me."

"Don't you think an attorney would be the better choice?"

"Perhaps," he said as he bent down and pulled out a roll of duct tape. As soon as he stood back up, he was upon Sam.

"What are you doing?" she yelled, but those were the last words she would be able to yell. Because he quickly taped her mouth with a double bound. She was screaming and fighting vigorously, but all to no effect. He then taped her hands together, and her legs.

That was easy enough, he thought, as he lifted her up and carried her into the small bedroom. He tossed her onto the bed, her small body wiggling like a fish out of water as soon as he dropped her down. He went back into the living room, grabbed his carrying bag, and returned to the bedroom. His bag of goodies included a rope, the duct tape, and a gun.

He began to use that rope, tying Sam's hands to the bed post and her feet together. Duct taping her mouth twice again just in case her screams could be heard before he had a chance to complete his mission. Because, he knew, his biggest task lay ahead of him.

But not far ahead, he thought, as he heard footsteps on the stairs again, and Jade's sometimes nauseating voice in the silence.

"Markie, where are you?" she said in that sing-song, valley girl way of hers. How some South Carolina, country-ass girl like her could get a voice like that was a mystery to him. Not that he dwelt on that mystery, however. He didn't dwell on it at all. He, instead, grabbed his bag of goodies as if it were a bag of his clothes, headed out of the bedroom, and closed the door behind him. Obstacle Number One, Samantha Redding, easily adverted and secured. Now he was face to face with Obstacle Number Two.

"What are you doing?" Jade asked as soon as she saw that tote bag in his hand.

"What do you think?" he moved past her, near the sofa where he planned to put her down.

"Daddy doesn't own this house. He can't make you leave."

"But you're leaving," he said, sitting down on the sofa, his tote bag at his feet. "You're going back to Carolina with your mother."

"No, I'm not!" Jade said defiantly, moving toward him. "That's what she thinks I'm doing, but I'm not. I want us to be together." She sat down, on his lap, wrapped her hands around his neck. "Don't you want to be with me?"

Marcus smiled. He'd rather have alligators in his bed than her obnoxious ass. "Of course I want to be with you," he said, smiling that charming smile of his again. "Right now, in fact."

Jade smiled. "You love doing me, don't you?"

Marcus reached down, pulled the gun out of his bag. "I do," he said. "Only this time, I want to add a little spice to your nice."

"Mom's upstairs somewhere. She might tipped down here again the way she did last night."

"And?" Marcus said with a smile. "She'll enjoy the show, I assure you." Then he placed the gun at the side of Jade's head. Jade's eyes stretched in shock.

"What are you doing, Marcus?" she asked hysterically, her eyes trying desperately to see what it was pressed against her.

Marcus almost smiled. There was nothing he liked about this heifer. "I'm getting what's mine, babe, that's all," he said. "Now you can either cooperate with me, or you can see your brains splattered all over this cute little sofa. And then, it'll be mama's turn."

Tears began to appear in Jade's eyes. "Mama? My mama?"

"Now if you cooperate, everybody keeps living with their brains intact." He pressed the gun harder against her. "It's up to you."

"Okay!" she said nervously, careful to not set him off. "What-what do you want me to do?"

"Pull out your cell phone."

"I don't have it with me. I think I left it at the Residence."

"Then you're one dead motherfucker then, because I need you to use your cell phone. Pull it out!" he screamed and Jade quickly pulled it out of the inside flap of the jacket she wore. Marcus knew her too well. He knew exactly where Jade kept that phone of hers.

"Ah, you have some sense after all," he said when the phone appeared. "Now," he went on, "I want you to call Daddy."

Jade's heart began to pound even harder. "Why?"

"I want you to tell Daddy that Mom's acting crazy again, and you need him to get over here. Tell him it can't wait. You need him to come. One thing about your old daddy, he comes when his precious little girl calls. And if you value your life, you'd better make sure he comes this time. So make it convincing, Jade. One false move and I shoot you, the old lady, and your fucking daddy. So don't fuck this up, girl." Marcus made sure they made eye contact. "I mean it."

Jade stared at him, terror in her eyes.

Dutch and Gina were out on the Truman Balcony, sitting side by side in loungers, still decompressing from that meeting this morning, when the phone call came in. Gina sipped juice and listened as Dutch spoke with his daughter. She, undoubtedly, wanted him to come over to her house again. This, Gina feared, was beginning to be a consistent theme. Use any excuse to get him away from Gina and with her and that mother of hers. When he hung up, Gina could tell he knew it, too.

"Let me guess," she said. "Sam's supposedly all confused and nutty again, and Jade wants you over there."

"Bingo," he said. "Another one of her pathetic ploys to get me and Sam back together."

Gina smiled. "That's so ridiculous. Do you truly think Jade believes you'll just leave me like that?"

"She believes whatever she wants to believe. Forget the reality of the situation. That, perhaps, is what concerns me most about her."

"You said you were going to hook her up with Dr. Katz."

"I have. And Dr. Katz has agreed to start seeing her."

"But she hasn't agreed?"

"Not yet, no," Dutch admitted. "She's certain she's fine. But yet she goes around screwing Marcus right under her husband's nose, cowering down to her mother as if she was still some kid terrified of her, and calling me in some twisted ploy to get me away from you."

"But I still don't understand it," Gina said. "Doesn't she realize that you and her mother had a one-night stand? It wasn't any great love to begin with."

"She knows the story. I told it to her. Sam's told it to her. Repeatedly. Yet she still wants me to leave you and to be with her mother."

"I think she wants you to leave me, all right," Gina said carefully, "but I'm not so sure it's her mother she wants you to be with. I suspect, I could be wrong, but I suspect baby girl wants you for herself."

Dutch's heart began to pound. Could his daughter be that messed up? He had been urging her to meet with the therapist. He had even offered to sit in on a few sessions with her. But all of his efforts were to no avail. Now he might just have to force the issue. He did it with Gina last year. He might have to do it with Jade.

"Anyway," he said, refusing to even entertain Gina's theory, "she insists that I come, and that I come now."

"But you have to be on Capitol Hill in fifteen minutes. Why didn't you just tell her that?"

"I started to, but then I realized what good would that do? She'll just insist that I come after my meeting on the Hill." He looked at Gina. "I want you to go."

Gina looked at him. "Me?"

"Yes. I want Jade to realize, once and for all, that you represent me. There's nothing wrong with Sam. You know it and I know it. Sam will always be Sam. Jade knows it too. So go over there, prove to her that her little attention grabs won't be grabbing us any longer, check on Sam who, I'm certain, is just fine. And hopefully she'll get the message."

"Whether she does or not I do want to talk with Marcus," Gina said. "I want to see what his plans are. Because Jade, as you know, isn't hardly going back to no South Carolina with Sam. She is not about to leave her beloved daddy. But I don't want Marcus there any longer."

Dutch looked at her. "Were you surprised that he and Jade had hooked up?"

"Goodness, yes. I was stunned. Jade and my brother? It seemed wrong. But then again, after I heard them talk, I realized just how it wasn't ridiculous at all. They deserve each other to tell you the truth. It's Chris I'm most concerned about."

Dutch nodded. "He'll be okay. He just needs a certain kind of woman."

"What kind of woman is that?" Gina asked. Dutch always had a warm spot in his heart for Christian. He always wanted the best for him.

"I can't pinpoint it exactly," Dutch said. "But he certainly needs somebody who realizes his worth. Somebody the polar opposite of that daughter of mine." Then he stood up. "I'd better get going," he said. "The Speaker of the House awaits my presence."

"Lucky Speaker," Gina said with a smile as Dutch leaned down and kissed her.

But then he lingered there, looking her in the eyes, a look of fright suddenly appearing in his own eyes.

"What is it?" Gina asked, startled by his change in expression.

Dutch didn't know what it was exactly. Just a sudden feeling that came quickly and left just as fast. "It was just. . . nothing." He stood erect, still looking pensive. Mainly because he couldn't even verbalize what that momentary feeling really was. "Anyway, you take care of yourself." Then he thought again. "Maybe we'll do something tonight," he said. "You, me, and Little Walt. We might even go back to the house in Arlington."

Gina smiled grandly. "Oh, Dutch, really? That would be fantastic!"

"Then consider it done. Set it up. You're becoming good at that sort of thing." Gina laughed. "Bye, babe," he said, looked at her once more, and then headed off of the balcony and straight for that enemy territory they called Capitol Hill.

It was accomplished. Jade was in the basement, bound and gagged, and Sam was in the basement, bound and gagged too. Obstacle one and two handled. The phone call had been made and the trap was set. Beautifully set, if Marcus had to say so himself. The assault rifle was rigged and facing the mud room doorway. The only way into the home from the garage was the mud room. The only way into the living area was through the mud room. The door was always unlocked as it was the entrance reserved for the Secret Service, whenever necessary, and the president. Dutch always had to enter from that particular entrance.

Marcus had it ready for him, too. He would enter the home from the garage, walk along the small, narrow mud room, and then he had to walk under the archway to get into the living area. And as soon as he crossed the threshold of that archway, the trigger would release, bullets would fly, and Dutch Harber, Marcus thought with unbridled satisfaction, would be as dead as Marcus felt alive.

Marcus, in fact, felt as if he was on Cloud Nine. He was even smiling when he left the home. He spoke to Benny, the agent on street-side duty, got into his car parked on the street, and left. He was headed for the private jet Thurston Osgood had waiting for him. He would be on that jet and out of

DC within minutes. He would be offshore shortly thereafter. And his millions would be deposited into his South American bank account, under his assumed name and new identity, as soon as the media reported the fall of Dutch Harber.

Marcus hit the steering wheel as he turned another corner and made his getaway, laughing all the way. It felt exhilarating. It felt freeing. It felt as if he was stealing Da Vinci's Mona Lisa, Rembrandt's Night Watch, and Michelangelo's David, all in broad daylight.

Crader McKenzie stood to his feet as soon as the door to his office opened. His secretary had said that his wife was there to see him, and he had urged her to send her through. He had wanted to scream at that secretary for not sending her through without asking permission, but he didn't want more negative energy surrounding him and LaLa than there already was.

LaLa entered the office unsure why she was even there. Especially after what she did with Christian.

"Hey," Crader said, attempting to smile, although his heart was hammering. "I was just trying to sign more documents. Sometimes I think that's the only job Dutch wants me doing: signing the papers he doesn't want to sign." He chuckled at his own joke. But then he realized LaLa was just standing there, tears appearing in her eyes.

"What's wrong?" he asked nervously as he hurried from around his desk and made his way to her side. She shook her head, but could not speak.

"Oh, babe," he said, rubbing her arm, tears in his own eyes. "I'm so sorry. I never meant to hurt you, you've got to believe that. I wasn't thinking. I was just doing. I never meant to hurt you! Please believe that, La."

La looked at him. "I believe it," she said. "After what I did, I believe you."

Crader didn't know what she meant, but he pulled her into his arms. *After what she did*, he thought as he held her. What was that supposed to mean? What had she done? Was another man involved? Had his stupid actions sent his wife into the arms of another man?

He closed his eyes, terrified.

Dear Lord, he thought. *What have I done?*

Dutch stood in Statuary Hall on the southern end of the Capitol Rotunda and listened intensely. The introduction was long and drawn out, he hadn't expected any less from the verbose Speaker of the House. It was no secret that the Speaker loved the limelight. He loved it so much that he had taken what should have been a simple introduction of the president and turned it into a soliloquy on bipartisanship and committee assignments. Allison Shearer, who stood beside the president, leaned over to him.

"This is going to be a long day," she whispered.

"It already is," Dutch whispered back, prompting Allison to smile.

The audience, which largely consisted of House committee chairmen, seemed fascinated by their leader's speech. But the last thing on Dutch's mind was any of these people or their political ambitions. He was still antsy, for some reason, he still hadn't been able to shake that feeling of dread he felt earlier. He leaned toward Allison.

"Ally," he said, and she moved closer. "Do me a favor and call the Nursery. Make sure Little Walt's okay."

"Yes, sir," she replied.

"And also phone my wife's cell," he continued. "Tell her I was just thinking about her."

Allison looked at Dutch. He wasn't a hovering kind of husband. He knew Gina wouldn't like that. But he was the boss. "Yes, sir," she said, and stepped outside of the room to do as he ordered.

The dark SUV, windows tinted, drove into the garage at Jade and Christian's home not unlike the numerous other times this same vehicle had done so before. Only this time the president and First Lady wasn't in the backseat, but the First Lady alone.

The driver was her usual bodyguard, a Secret Service agent, and the female on the front passenger side was also a member of the Secret Service. They both got out of the vehicle as soon as it stopped, with one, the male, moved to open the truck's back door, while the female agent headed for the door of the home.

Gina, in an attractive puce-colored pantsuit, stepped out of the SUV and made her way toward the home's entrance. The female agent opened the door and allowed her passage in. It was always the routine, as worked out when Dutch purchased the home for his daughter and son-in-law.

"Thanks, Carla," Gina said as she entered the home's mud room just off from the garage. The door was closed, leaving Gina inside, the agents outside. That was the protocol. They never entered the personal space of the First Family unless specifically asked, or if they suspected distress.

Gina's cell phone chirped as soon as she entered the mud room. She looked at the screen. It was Allison. She stopped walking and immediately answered.

"Ally, hi," she said with a smile. She and Allison were becoming very good friends. "What's up, doc?"

"The president told me to phone you and let you know that he was thinking about you."

"Oh, that's so sweet," Gina said with a smile. But it wasn't exactly like Dutch to ask somebody else to phone her with such a personal message. "Is he okay?"

"He's fine. He's stuck listening to the Speaker give one of his long-behind speeches."

Gina laughed. "Well tell the president that I'm thinking about him, too."

"Where are you," Allison asked, "because I'm sure he's going to want to know?"

"I just arrived at Jade's. Tell him I'm fine."

"Good enough," Allison said. "I'll let him know."

Then Gina said her goodbyes and killed the call.

Earlier, just as Gina was entering the mud room, Jade was freeing herself. Marcus had taped her mouth and bound her wrists and ankles, as she had done with Sam, and tossed Jade in the room with her mother and closed the door. Jade had managed to wiggle her way from the bottom of the bed to the top, where her mother was able to work feverishly to free her hands.

And now it was finally working. Jade's rope began to loosen just enough for her to squeeze her small hands through. She then untied the rope from her ankles and removed the tape from her mouth, the pain of the removal excruciating. And although Sam was motioning for Jade to loosen her ropes, too, Jade was up and running.

"I've got to warn Daddy!" she yelled as she ran, horror in her voice. "I've got to warn Daddy!"

She slung open the bedroom door, ran up the basement stairs, flung open the basement door, and was about to scream for help when she heard Gina's voice, in the mud room, telling someone that she had just arrived. Jade then looked to her side and saw the assault rifle. She saw that it was rigged. She saw how it was facing the entrance in the mud room that led into the living room. Then she heard Gina say goodbye to whomever she was talking to, and then she heard footsteps. Gina was heading toward the living area.

Jade could have warned her. Jade could have told her to wait and to not take another step. She could have told her that danger was just around that corner!

But she froze.

She didn't say a word.

And Regina Harber, the First Lady of the United States, rounded that corner and entered that living room the way she had rounded that corner and entered that living room so many times before, as nothing at all was different about this time. She even smiled when she saw Jade standing there.

"Hello there," she said as soon as she crossed the threshold.

But as soon as she crossed that threshold, the assault rifle fired in rapid succession, fired all five shots as it was rigged to do. Only five shots proved to be overkill. Because Gina was already going down, the blood already gushing out, by the time the third bullet sailed toward her like a bolt of lightning, and ripped through her body.

Jade's body tensed up during the firing. And relaxed beyond measure when it was all over, and the Secret Service had arrived.

CHAPTER FIFTEEN

Dutch was now at the podium, answering questions from a member of the Republican leadership. Why, this leader wanted to know, was the White House dragging its feet on the debt ceiling amendment? Dutch was about to answer, although everybody in the room knew the guy was trying to put the blame for congressional gridlock on the president. But just as Dutch was about to place blame where it truly belonged, the Secret Service agent in charge burst into the room in a dead run, a team of agents running behind him.

"You need to come with us, sir," the agent said as he grabbed the president by the arm, not waiting for an answer, and began running him out of the room.

"What's happened?" Dutch was asking as they ran, with Allison right behind him, but nobody was answering. The agents were too busy talking in their earpieces, securing the Rotunda, getting POTUS safely away. There was a shooting and the shooters, for all they knew, could be gunning for the president next.

The Speaker and his committee chairmen were running out of Statuary Hall, behind the agents, wondering what in the world was going on.

It wasn't until Dutch and Allison were shoved into the back of the waiting limousine, and Ralph Shaheen, the head of the Secret Service, was getting in with them, did the president himself find out anything at all.

"What the fuck's going on here, Shaheen?!" Dutch roared angrily as the limo sped off in a blur of burned rubber. Congressmen and staffers alike were running out of the Rotunda to see what was going on. They had never seen the president whisked away anything like that. It was obvious to them that something had happened, and something big.

Ralph Shaheen exhaled first, and then spoke haltingly. "It's the First Lady, sir," he said.

Dutch's heart stalled. He couldn't will himself to feel, to think, to dread anything. Or to breathe. Until he spoke her name.

"Gina?" he asked.

"Yes, sir."

"What about Gina?" His voice sounded distant, almost faint.

Even Ralph, Allison realized, looked devastated. "She's been shot, sir," he said, and Dutch's heart took in a harsh inhale. And then a harsher release.

"Shot?" he said, his face a mask of anguish. "Gina's been shot?"

"Yes, sir. They're airlifting her to Bethesda right now."

"But . . ." Dutch couldn't wrap his brain around this. His face was a mask of anguish. "You're telling me that Gina, that my wife. . . That

Gina's been shot?" This sounded untrue to Dutch. Unreal.

"Yes, sir," Ralph replied. "The First Lady has been shot."

"But she's all right?" Dutch had the look of a child seeking approval. It broke Allison's heart.

Ralph glanced at Allison. Then he looked back at the president. "She's still alive, sir," was all he was willing to say about it.

"What do you mean she's still alive?" Dutch snapped. "Of course she's still alive! Why would you make a statement like that?"

"Because it's true, Dutch!" Ralph said. He and Dutch were old friends. And although he was not a political figure, and had a very non-personal role to play as head of the Secret Service, this was personal with him now. Somebody shot his good friend's wife on his watch. This was personal. "She's fighting for her life," he said.

Dutch stared at his old friend, but he was still unable to fully appreciate the words he spoke. Then he ran his hand across his face. This couldn't be happening. He just knew this could not possibly be happening, not to Gina. Not Gina!

"What did it . . . How did it . . . What happened, Ralph?"

"She went to visit Jade, who, incidentally, is okay thank God."

"What happened to Gina?" Dutch asked impatiently. Although a part of him was naturally pleased to hear that Jade was fine, he didn't want

DUTCH AND GINA 6

to hear about anybody else right now. He *couldn't* hear about anybody else right now. "Tell me what happened to my wife!" he ordered.

"She went over to Jade's house," Ralph continued, "and there was a trap apparently set for her."

A frown appeared on Dutch's face. "A trap? What kind of trap?"

"A gun, an assault rifle, had been rigged to fire on her entry into the home."

"Good Lord," Dutch said, running his hand through his hair, his heart hammering.

"It was rigged to fire five rounds," Ralph went on. "And it did."

"*Five times*?" Dutch asked amazed. "She was shot *five times*?"

"Three solid hits, one graze, and one complete miss, sir. Four of the five bullets did hit."

Dutch ran his hand across his face again. He felt as if he was in quicksand. Slowly sinking. "Who would do such a thing?" he asked in an almost rhetorical question to no-one, his eyes trailing around the car.

"We believe, sir," Ralph said, "that Mr. Rance is responsible."

Dutch looked at Ralph. "Marcus?"

"Yes, sir."

"You believe her own brother did this to her?"

Allison covered her mouth in shock, tears already in her eyes. Ralph nodded his head. "Yes, sir," he said.

Dutch shook his head. "Where is he?" he asked. "Where is that sonafabitch?!"

"We don't. . . we don't know where he is, sir. But we're searching."

Dutch frowned. "You mean to tell me that asshole was able to shoot my wife four times and walk away from it?"

"He set the trap first, sir, and then he left. But we'll find him, I promise you that. We had no idea." Ralph was looking almost as distressed as Dutch. "We were right outside the door, sir. Protocol did not allow us to go inside that home without a reason or invitation. We had no idea what Rance had done until we heard the rapid fire. We arrived immediately, immediately, sir. But the First Lady was already down."

Dutch closed his eyes. The idea of Gina down, with bullets riddled through her body, punctured his heart. He wasn't there to protect her. He wasn't there to shield her. He wasn't there! And it was unbearable to Dutch. Unbearable like a nightmare. He wanted out of this nightmare. He wanted to wake up from this!

Then he thought about his son. His innocent, defenseless son. He opened his eyes. "What about Little Walt?" he asked, panic surging within him. "You've got to take me to Little Walt!"

"He's fine, sir," Ralph assured him. "We've shut down the White House and secured the Nursery. Walter Harber, Junior is in our complete protective custody, sir," Ralph made clear. "The nannies do not even have access to him right now."

Dutch exhaled. He knew he had to pull it together. Then he thought beyond Walt and Gina. "You said Jade was okay?"

"Jade is fine, yes, sir. She nor her mother were harmed. Jade, in fact, insisted on being airlifted with the First Lady."

Dutch thought about Jade. He thought about her sometimes stinging resentment of Gina. He looked at Ralph. "Watch her," he said.

This edict confused Ralph. "Sir?"

"I didn't stutter. You watch that young lady. You call your agents on that helicopter right now and you tell them to watch Jade. You tell them that I don't want her anywhere near my wife right now."

Ralph glanced at Allison. What was he talking about?

"You heard me!" Dutch roared. "Contact your people! I don't want Jade, or Sam, or anybody else near my wife right now. It may sound cruel to you, and I may sound heartless toward my own child, but I don't give a fuck how it sounds. I don't know if they had a hand in this trap that was set for Gina or not, and I'm not taking any chances." My sorry ass had already taken too many chances, Dutch wanted to add. He'd already ignored too many clues that were staring him in the face!

"Yes, sir," Ralph said nervously, and began making contact with the agents that were in full escort of the First Lady's body.

Crader sat on the sofa and waited for LaLa to talk to him. She had said she understood him now, especially after what she had done, and then she sat him down to tell him what it was exactly that she had done. Only she couldn't find the words to tell him.

Not that he wanted to know. He didn't. Unfair as it seemed, given what he had done, a big part of him didn't think he could handle the thought of another man touching his wife. But he knew he had to know. He had to know if his actions drove his wife into the arms of another man.

"I could never be in love with someone," LaLa began, "and then allow another man to touch me. That's what I've always said. That's how I've always led my life. I couldn't understand how you could have slept with another woman, or even flirted with another woman, if you truly loved me. I just couldn't believe it was possible."

Crader stared at her. "But you believe it's possible now?"

LaLa was too ashamed to look him in the eyes. "Yes," she said with a frown on her face.

"What happened, La?" he asked her.

But the agony LaLa felt almost paralyzed her.

"Tell me," Crader insisted. "It's bad. I already know it's bad."

That declaration, that he was already suspecting the worse, helped her to face him. She looked at him. "I was. . . home and thinking about what all I had to do today. I wasn't expecting. . . I didn't expect it to happen."

"You didn't expect what to happen? Tell me, love. Just tell me."

"I never dreamed I would . . . I could . . ."

"Who's the guy?" Crader suddenly had to know.

But LaLa was still too involved in her own share of the blame to even think about pointing a finger at someone else.

"Tell me, La. Who's the guy?"

The door to the office of the vice president flung open so hard it bounced back from its hinges. Christian Bale, his face white as a sheet, ran in.

Crader jumped to his feet. LaLa was dazed. Had he heard their conversation?

"What is it?" Crader wanted to know.

But Christian couldn't speak. He just stood there. Then he ran to the table, grabbed the remote, and turned on the television. It didn't matter what channel. Christian knew it was live on every channel.

Crader and LaLa immediately looked at the television, too.

"...has been shot," the news anchor was in the middle of saying as soon as the TV clicked on. "I repeat, the First Lady of the United States, Regina

Harber, has been severely wounded in a hail of gunfire inside her stepdaughter's home."

Crader's heart almost pounded out of his chest. LaLa placed her hand over her heart, to force herself to breathe. And Christian collapsed against the table, still unable to utter a mumbling word.

Marcus Rance poured himself a glass of bubbly and reclined on the private jet as it steered him further and further away from his homeland. He was ready to celebrate. It had gone better than he could have ever dreamed. It was such a clean getaway that he could hardly contain his joy.

And he had given it time. He had given it more than enough time to hit the airwaves. Now, as he relaxed, he finally clicked on the television set in front of him. And sure enough, he thought with a grin, it was breaking news.

"Nobody can believe it," the reporter was saying as he stood outside of the home Marcus once shared with Jade and Christian. "The blood, the carnage. According to our sources it was a horrific scene. Who could do such a thing, everyone's asking. Who would have shot to kill the First Lady?"

Marcus smiled turned into a frown. What was he talking about? The First Lady? Did he say the First Lady?

"But that was exactly what somebody had done," the reporter went on. "Authorities tell us that someone, and we believe they know who the suspect is, shot to kill Regina Harber, our First Lady, and they shot her four times."

The glass in Marcus's hand dropped involuntarily, and crashed to the floor.

The presidential motorcade arrived at the helipad to make the final leg of the journey to Bethesda Naval Hospital by chopper. Dutch and Allison were scurried out of the limo and onto the aircraft quickly, with a wall of agents on either side of them. They were seated, buckled in, and lifted away.

Dutch lobbed his head backwards, and wiped his eyes with the back of his hand, as emotional exhaustion began to overtake him. He felt as if he'd aged a hundred years in a matter of minutes. And talk about blame. Just before he was ushered out, he was in a meeting where Congress was pointing a finger at him, and he was pointing a finger at them, when everybody knew both were responsible for this economic mess. But Dutch knew, painfully, that he and he alone was responsible for this mess that his wife, that his precious Gina, found herself in.

He looked out of the window as Marine One careened across the sky on a beeline to its destination. Dutch knew he had nobody to blame but himself. He was the one who used political maneuverings to get Governor Feingold to grant Marcus Rance that pardon. He was the one who didn't stop Jade and Christian for taking Marcus into their home. He was the one who sent his wife to that firing squad, when, he realized, that fire was supposed to be for him. But to his everlasting shame, he had sent his wife to take the bullets for him.

When he felt that niggling feeling this morning he should have paid more attention to that. That feeling gripped him for a reason. But he ignored it. Just as he ignored the danger of life in a fishbowl for his wife and son. The day Little Walt was born should have been the day they left Washington. The day Gina was excoriated in the media, or when Walt was almost kidnapped, should have been his wake up calls. But oh no. Not the great Dutch Harber! He couldn't let his enemies win. He couldn't surrender to any of them. He had to see his ambitions through. And if it caused his wife to fight for her life this very day, well that was just the price of being associated with a man like him.

Dutch closed his eyes again.

As shame washed over him.

But he didn't stay in that state long. Because the helicopter landed, he and Allison were ushered out, and before he knew it he was inside Bethesda Naval Hospital running along corridor after corridor, to get to his wife.

Jade, who, along with Sam, were being politely but firmly detained by agents, broke free and ran to her father.

"Oh, Daddy!" she said as she threw her arms around him.

Dutch pulled her back and looked at his daughter as if he was looking at a stranger. But he couldn't blame her, either. His sins had been visited on her. He shared the blame for the hateful, selfish, hellish human being she'd become.

"It was awful, Daddy!" Jade said, looking her beautiful, hazel eyes up at him. "But it'll be okay. You have me and Ma. We'll take care of you."

Dutch looked at his gorgeous daughter, at the way she was already zeroing Gina out of the equation, and he hated what he saw. He hated it. God help him, he hated her. And he pushed her away from him.

"Where's my wife?" he said to his escorts, and the agents, once again, hurried him to the operating room. Allison was right behind them.

The chief of surgery was coming out of the O.R., removing his cap, as Dutch and his necessary entourage of agents came burrowing down the hall.

"Where is she?" Dutch demanded to know.

"She's being prepped for surgery, Mr. President."

Surgery, Dutch thought. Good Lord. "I've got to see her," he said, although he seemed to be talking beyond the doctor, and looking beyond the doctor. He was losing it. "I've got to let her know that she's going to be all right. She doesn't like hospitals, you see. She never has. She had pneumonia once, and I made her stay overnight in a hospital, and she just hated it. She never forgave me for that."

He was running his hand through his hair as he spoke. His hair was usually perfectly manicured. But now, like him, it was all over the place.

"I need to let her know that she's going to be all right, and that she'll be back home with me and Little Walt in the morning."

The surgeon looked at Allison. Was he for real, his expression said.

"Can I tell her that, Doc?" Dutch asked. "That'll make her feel better, you see, if you can promise me that she can come back home to us. Can I tell my wife that she'll be back home tomorrow?"

"Tomorrow?" the surgeon asked, shock in his voice. He understood trauma and he understood denial. But the president was experiencing overflow doses of both.

"Yes, tomorrow," Dutch said, knowing intellectually that he was slipping, but determined to go down with hope. "Can I tell Gina, can I tell my wife that she'll be back home with us tomorrow?"

The chief of surgery moved his body from side to side. This was damned uncomfortable even for a man of his esteem. But it had to be said.

"Mr. President," he said as kindly, but also as bluntly as he knew how, "it'll be the miracle of miracles if your wife makes it through the night."

It felt like a body blow. And it took the president's breath away.

He thought about Gina, and if he'd ever see her wonderful smile again. He thought about all the plans they had for life after the White House. He thought about her horrific cooking and her fantastic lovemaking and her beautiful heart. Her wonderful, beautiful heart. He thought about how she drove him to Virginia, away from the politics of DC, just to give him a moment's rest. He thought about Gina. And what life would be like without her.

This was his day of reckoning.

His sins had finally caught him wanting.

He fell on his knees.

EPILOGUE

"I'll bet you fifty bucks."

"A hundred and you're on."

"A hundred? On our salary? Fifty, man, fifty."

"Can I get in on this deal?" a third reporter chimed in. They were in the Brady Press Room inside the White House. An aide had already alerted the jam-packed media that the president would come out first to make a statement, and then the press secretary would continue with his normal daily briefing. Speculation about just what the president was going to say filled the crowded room.

"What's the bet, anyway?" the third reporter asked.

"Carl here says the president will announce that there's been an agreement with House Republicans on the debt ceiling compromise. But I say the president is coming to announce that they tracked down Marcus Rance."

"But they haven't tracked down Marcus Rance," the third reporter reminded him.

"How do you know?"

"Because it would have leaked by now. It hasn't leaked because it hasn't happened."

"Ladies and gentlemen," the intercom announcer blared, "the President of the United States."

The reporters rose to their feet as the president entered the room from the back, and made his way up to the front. He was dressed in his usual expensive, tailored suit, but something was off this time. It wasn't its usual pristine elegance, but looked almost rumpled. The suave, debonair Dutch Harber, in fact, looked a little rumpled too, as if he'd been through hell and back again. Which, every reporter in the room would have to acknowledge, was factually accurate.

It had been nearly a month after that fateful day, and it was Dutch's first day officially back on the job. The American people had been patient with their president, allowing him time to get his act together, and Crader McKenzie had been holding down the fort just fine. But the press was growing antsy. They wanted Dutch. They wanted to hear from their president again. Now, nearly a month later, he was finally obliging them. And they all came ready, as usual, to devour him.

Although Dutch had a prepared statement, he knew almost instantly that he wasn't going to use it. He stood alone behind the podium, and stared out at the hundreds of questioning eyes that were staring back at him.

"I had a prepared speech that I was going to come out here and give to you," he began. "I was going to talk about the wonderful American people and how honored I have been to serve this nation. I was going to praise the media, for your hard-hitting journalism, and my fellow politicians for their commitment to their constituencies back home. I was going to come out here and lay it on thick. I wanted to be positive, you see. I wanted to move forward on a positive note. But in order to do so I would have to lie my head off, and I'm not going to do that."

The reporters in the room could sense combat. The old feisty Dutch Harber, they believed, was about to roar.

Dutch, however, was determined to keep it brief and get out of there. "The American people," he continued, "have been sold a bill of goods here in Washington. We have told them that all they have to do is work hard and play by the rules and that pot of gold is waiting for them, too. And I don't fault the politicians for selling that snake oil. I don't even fault the media for allowing us to sell it. I fault the American people for buying it. Year in and year out. From both parties. Time and time again. That's why nothing gets done in Washington. Because it's easier to sell the snake oil. It's easier to convince people that you have all the answers when you don't even know what the questions are."

Dutch hesitated. The reporters stared at him. "But if the American people would have stopped this nonsense, and held us accountable, then things could have gotten done. But there's no accountability. They're elections. But all we do is crown the guy with the best campaign ads or the one promising to come to Washington to obstruct the president's agenda. To do, in essence, absolutely nothing."

Dutch paused again. And then he continued. "I hate this place," he said. "I hate it with a passion. I don't dislike it, I hate it. I hate what I've become in this place, and I hate what I've allowed to happen in this place." Another pause, this one palpable. "Effective immediately," he said to amazement from a crowd that didn't see this coming, "I'm resigning as President of the United States."

The gasps of shock went out like thunderbolts in the room.

"Those of you who will be disappointed by my decision," Dutch went on, "I'm apologize for disappointing you. But I can't do this anymore. I can't do it. I can't slap another back or kiss another baby or pretend I'm actually doing good when all I'm doing is holding a spot until the next spot holder comes along. But what happened to my wife was a game changer. What happened to my wife was beyond enough. I can't put a positive spin on that kind of evil. I'm out of here. Some will cry, some will rejoice, I don't give a damn. I'm out of here."

And Dutch Harber walked out of the Brady Press Room for the very last time. There was silence. Shocking silence. And then the White House correspondents and the rest of the media, mainstream and backroom, went haywire.

There was no entourage of aides and other staffers waiting for Dutch outside the press room. Just LaLa, at his request.

"It's done?" she asked.

"It's done," he said. Then he put his arm around her and they began that slow trek down the corridors of power. For Dutch it would be his last walk this way.

"How do you feel?" she asked him.

Dutch didn't have to think about it. "Relieved," he said.

"It's been a tough road sometimes, Dutch, but you handled it all beautifully. Especially after what they did to Gina."

Dutch's heart squeezed at the mention of her name. "If it wasn't for you and Cray I don't know what I would have done. And Sam was a big help, too."

"She surprised me. She's not as oddball as people think when you really get down to it. But that daughter of yours, now that's another story."

"I know. She's with Sam now. But I don't know how long that'll last."

"For her to tell that reporter that Gina got what she deserved was a crying shame. I never thought Jade could be like that."

Dutch knew she harbored resentment against Gina, but he, too, never dreamed it had been that severe. Besides, he still wasn't at all certain that she didn't have a hand in what happened to Gina. That was why he hadn't spoken to his daughter since the tragedy. And wasn't sure when he could again.

"At least she's with her mother," LaLa said. "She can handle her."

It was the monster Sam created, with an assist from him, so she understood her. He wasn't so sure, however, if she could still handle her. She'd crossed the line when she made that public statement about Gina. He could never cut her off entirely, and maybe, in time, they could reestablish a relationship. But not now.

"Oh, well," Dutch said, as they continued their slow walk. "Life goes on."

"Yes, indeed. Many of the reporters were expecting you to announce that Marcus Rance had been found, if you can believe that."

"That would have made my day."

"Mine too, Dutch. Then maybe we could find out the whole truth. Why would he target his own sister when she was the only person who believed in him? And he could tell us if he acted alone."

"He'd better hope the government finds him first, is all I have to say about it. Because if my men find him, and I have a team of them searching too, he won't have time to say much of anything."

LaLa laughed, certain that Dutch was kidding. Dutch, however, didn't crack a smile.

They were about to turn the corner that would lead them toward the South Portico. Dutch pulled LaLa back.

"Before I take my leave and say goodbye to the others, I just wanted to tell you how much I appreciate all you've done for me, Loretta. I don't think I could have made it without you."

LaLa smiled. She touched the side of Dutch's handsome, but worn, face. This man had gone through so much. He deserved some peace now.

"My only regret," he continued, "was that it had to take such an awful tragedy to get me to this place." Tears welled up in his eyes. "I should have taken my family away from this city a long time ago. When Little Walt was born in that hospital in Newark, I should have submitted my resignation as I sat in that hospital room. Maybe then Gina. . ."

LaLa hugged him, tears now in her eyes. "It's okay, Dutch," she said. "You can't look back. You served your country as best as you could, and that's all anybody could ask of you. That's all you can ask of yourself."

They stopped embracing. Dutch stared at her, smiled at her, and then gave her a kiss on the lips.

"You're a champ, you know that?" he said to her.

"A champ in my own mind," LaLa replied with laughter.

Dutch chuckled too. Then he looked at her again. "Let's turn the page a bit, shall we? I understand you're still staying at your house in Georgetown."

LaLa exhaled. That wasn't just another page they were turning. That was another book altogether. "For now," she said.

"You've stood by Crader during this whole ordeal. I was a basket case and he was essentially running the country even before I resigned. And you were right there with him. Even after the DNA results confirmed that that baby is his, you stood by him. You're to be commended for that, Loretta. Many women wouldn't do it."

"Yeah, well, it wasn't as altruistic as it seemed. I'm no better than Crader. We all fall short."

"Amen to that," Dutch agreed. Then he rubbed her arms, contemplatively looking into her eyes. "Christian is a good young man," he said. "I love him to death. But even with your husband's disastrous faults, and he has many, Christian is no Crader McKenzie."

LaLa stared at Dutch. Did he know about what she did with Christian? They both had agreed that they would never tell it to anyone. Crader knew she messed up with someone, but she never told him with whom. And, given his new responsibilities and the care he was taking in keeping this family together, albeit barely, he wasn't asking anymore. So who told Dutch, she wondered.

"Nobody told me," Dutch said, when he saw the baffled look in her eyes. "Nobody had to tell me. Crader had mentioned there were some issues in that direction, another man perhaps, but he didn't know who. I just happened to see the gleam that came into Christian's eyes whenever he mentioned your name."

LaLa shook her head. "That boy," she said, prompting Dutch to laugh as they began their final walk toward the exit.

Crader and Christian stood across from each other as they, along with all of the senior aides and cabinet secretaries, waited for the president in the corridor just inside the South Portico. It had been a long month. Crader was catapulted from the vice president who signed documents all day, into the lead role while Dutch stepped back and recovered. Although the DNA test confirmed that Crader was the father of Elvelyn's baby, and he still didn't know who LaLa had had an affair with, the stress of taking on a hundred more duties, with LaLa at his side, changed them. They could not look back. His mistakes, her mistakes, were to be for another day. Time did not permit them to focus on anything other than holding it down while Dutch got it together.

And now this.

Dutch met with them the night before and informed them of his decision, propelling Crader into the presidency with the stroke of a pen. The shock was still there for Crader, as he stood along that wall waiting to see Dutch Harber off. The thought that he was now responsible for running the entire government, that he was now the leader of the free world, was as terrifying as it was exhilarating.

Dutch and LaLa appeared in the corridor and the entire hall began to applaud. Dutch struck a tall, elegant pose as LaLa held back and he made that solitary walk for the last time. He walked lighter now, even more sure-footed, as he approached his friends and colleagues with hugs and kisses.

It took a long time, but he eventually made it out onto the south lawn, Crader at his side, as the entire White House staff, hundreds strong, applauded him.

Christian stood beside LaLa at the entrance door, and watched as the new president escorted the former president to the helipad. It was a passing of the baton, and the press would later play it up that way, but Dutch was thrilled to pass it on.

Christian looked at LaLa. "You're the new First Lady now," he said.

The idea of it still stunned LaLa. "Yes, that's true."

Christian immediately saw her differently. But he still couldn't help his feelings. "Jade finally signed the divorce papers," he said.

LaLa looked at him. "You're okay with that?"

"It's what I wanted, yes," he said. Then he paused. "What about you, and Senator, I mean Vice, I mean President McKenzie?"

LaLa looked at Crader, as he and Dutch talked at the helicopter. "I'm going to hold on, Chris," she said, "and see what the end is going to be."

Christian's heart dropped. "But he cheated on you, La."

"I cheated on him."

"It's not the same."

LaLa looked at Christian. He looked so young to her, right then and there. "Yes, it is the same," she corrected him.

"But you don't have to stay. Why are you staying in such a troubled marriage?"

LaLa started to give the usual reasons people stayed: because she loved him, because he was the father of her baby girl. But she thought about what Dutch had said. "Because he needs me," she said, instead.

Christian had to think about this. And then he responded. "But what do you need, La?"

La thought about this. "To be needed," she admitted.

It would not be long before the chopper landed on the back side of the Harber estate in Newark, New Jersey. Dutch stepped off, saluted the pilot one last time, and made his way across the property. It was a gorgeous piece of land, with a lakeside view that seemed panoramic. But the best view of all for Dutch was when he walked along the home's colonnade, onto the front side of the property, and saw his wife and son playing catch on the lawn. And when they saw that Dutch had returned to them, they took off running for him.

Dutch stood there, in awe. He couldn't help himself. This was what life was about to him. Not being the most powerful man in the world, or commanding attention just by walking into the room. But to see the smile he put on the faces of his family just by coming home, was pure happiness to him.

He swept Little Walt up into his arms, and then he placed his arm around Gina, lifting her too. But they weren't heavy. They were his responsibility. And he embraced them heartily.

"I saw it on TV," Gina said as she swept his hair out of his face. "You looked great."

Dutch looked at her. She wasn't a hundred percent yet, but she was close. No permanent damage, at least not physically. "And how are you doing, young lady?" he asked her.

"I feel wonderful, Dutch. Glad to have you back."

"Glad to be back," he said.

Early in her rehab she used to ask him, every night, if they had found Marcus Rance yet. And every night he had to tell her no. But time was a wonderful ally. Dutch had hired the best investigators he could find. Time would find that bastard. And then he would have an appointment with Dutch.

"It's getting chilly out," Dutch said, walking his family toward the entrance. "Let's go inside."

Gina smiled. "I'll race you," she said, and took off running.

"Not fair," Dutch said, running behind her. "I have a kid in my arms!"

"Run, Mommy, run!" Little Walt said as he grinned at his parents.

And Gina ran. It warmed Dutch's heart to see just how beautifully Gina ran.

Now was the beginning of their new life together. No fishbowls, no spotlights, just them. And Dutch, like Gina, couldn't wait to get started.

AUSTIN BROOK PUBLISHING

For more information and updates Visit
www.austinbrookpublishing.com